ATLANTIS OBSESSION

ATLANTIS OBSESSION

RICHARD GARTEE

Lake and Emerald Publications

Portions of this book were previously released in serial form on Kindle Vella

Published by Lake & Emerald Publications, LLC

Gainesville, FL

www.lepublications.com

ISBN 978-1-7363957-4-5

Library of Congress Control Number: 2023918210

This is a work of fiction. Characters, places, and incidents are the product of the author's imagination. Referenced scientific papers discussed in the story are listed in the bibliography.

Front cover an original collage created from Unsplash photos by Eugene Tkachenko and Kal Visuals

Back cover photo: Eye of the Sahara courtesy of NASA

Typesetting services by BOOKOW.COM

For the peas: Allison, Bonnie, Pat, and Ken

RICHARD GARTEE

Acknowledgments

Thank you to fellow members of Writers Alliance of Gainesville who critiqued the book as I was writing it: Ken Campbell, Pat Caren, Allison Durham, and Bonnie Ogle; my editor Dave King; and proofreader: Pat Caren.

Chapter 1
Late Start

Dylan Clarke's phone alarm was thumping "Afterglow," Taylor Swift's breakup anthem—well, one of them. Groggy, he snatched it off the bed stand and fumbled for the off button. Not a good song to wake up to, especially in the middle of the dream he was having.

He rolled over and snuggled back into his pillow, determined to finish.

Holly, his former girlfriend, never looked better. She had eyes you could lose yourself in and a smile that stole his heart the first time she'd turned it on him. It didn't hurt that she had red hair like his, though hers was darker, a shade of red so deep it was almost brunette. And then he was back with her, in the dream, standing together on the rim of a caldera, where he was pointing out the circular canals surrounding Atlantis. . .

He jerked awake. Why hadn't the alarm gone off? He picked up his phone.

He was already an hour behind. Dammit.

Dylan stumbled into the bathroom, splashed water on his pale, freckled face, and ran his hand over his chin. The stubble was prickly but didn't show much. It took a few days for a five o'clock shadow to develop, one of the advantages of being a natural redhead. Shaving could wait.

He donned a light blue dress shirt, a clean pair of khaki slacks, black socks, and tassel loafers. Around his neck he draped an orange and blue striped tie with the university mascot embroidered on it—a birthday gift from Holly back when they were together. Normally, he didn't wear a tie, but his department was hosting a symposium on Worldwide Desertification of Arable Lands with scholars from around the nation and the world. As a doctoral candidate in climatology, he was expected to dress like them. Besides, he could make meaningful contacts this week. He brushed lint off his navy-blue blazer and put it on.

He checked the time on his phone, and found instead a series of texts, the gist of which were: "Where R U?" His duties included helping organize the conference. He'd been there until after midnight doing just that, one reason he'd slept so late. Of course, the other reason was, instead of going to sleep when he came home, he'd stayed up reading a book on Atlantis. He'd been doing a lot of research on the reality behind the myths, and he wanted to be sure of his facts for the day.

No time to eat. He dashed out, locked his apartment door, and jumped into his Honda. Dylan turned the key. The starter groaned, then whined, and then went silent. A second and third try resulted in a series of disappointing clicks.

No point calling road service. Who knew how long before they'd get here? The symposium was being held at the Hilton University of Florida Conference Center, which was only about fifteen blocks away. He raced back into the apartment and wrestled his bicycle from the laundry room where it had been stored for months. The tires seemed a little soft when he put his weight on the bike, but at least they weren't flat.

Halfway through the ride, he was sweating. He stopped, removed his blazer, folded it neatly, and tucked it into his backpack. So much for looking professional.

Fifteen minutes later, Dylan peddled up to the redbrick conference center, hungry as hell and hopelessly late. He locked his bike to a signpost, wiped the sheen of sweat from his face, and opened the glass door to the brightly lit, mostly empty, reception area. The attendees were already in the first sessions. A couple of undergrads tending the registration desk sat scrolling their iPhones.

It didn't matter. He'd helped prepare the agenda and knew which conference room he wanted. He pulled his blazer out of the backpack, shook out the wrinkles, sort of, and put it on.

Two busboys were clearing away pastry platters from the continental breakfast. "Wait!" he said in a stage whisper. They paused, but he was too late. Ravenous students had left nothing but crumbs.

Dylan carefully opened the door to the conference hall, slipped inside, and closed it slowly, so it wouldn't bang. Dr. Gujarat, his professor of paleoclimatology, was just concluding his introduction of Dr. Porter, the main speaker for this session. The room was full and the only remaining vacant seats were in the front row. Damn. No way could he slip in unseen. Oh well, better do it before Porter begins. At least he hadn't missed the lecture.

Chapter 2
A Wet Sahara

Dylan kept his head down as he slipped into a chair at the far end of the front row. This morning's speaker was the caricature of a British academic—short, rotund, bald with gray fringe. All he needed was a tweed jacket with patches on the sleeves. A PowerPoint presentation on the screen behind him had his name, Dr. Geoffrey Porter, in letters two-feet tall. Beneath that, slightly smaller: Kings College, London.

A little egocentric, but they'd been lucky to get him. No reason not to let him crow.

The man straightened his tie, stepped to the podium, and lowered the microphone. The sound system crackled, and the harsh rasp from adjusting the gooseneck echoed through the auditorium like a rusty hinge in a horror movie. "Sensitive little bugger."

The audience laughed.

Porter turned to Dr. Gujarat. "Thank you for that introduction and for inviting me to participate. I'd also like to thank President Sasse and the University of Florida for hosting this important conference on climate change. I'm glad you held it here. It's freezing back home in England."

A few in the audience tittered. Dylan only smiled.

Porter cleared his throat. "Other sessions at this conference are focusing on human enterprises that generate greenhouse gases, which are accelerating climate change much faster than ever before. And it is right to do so, for that is a factor we have a modicum of control over."

From his position in the front row, Dylan could see the professor fumbling around, looking for the little clicker that advanced the slides. He wondered if he should go up and help him. Just then, Porter found it under his papers. He pressed a button, and the screen displayed a collage of oil rigs, a stockyard crowded with cattle, and a logging operation clear-cutting a section of rainforest.

"Politicians who cling to the notion that global warming is a hoax are, as is increasingly obvious, dead wrong. Every last scientist at this conference agrees that global warming is contributing to expanding deserts. I hope this conference produces actionable scientific results that nations will take to heart."

The audience nodded so vigorously Dylan could almost hear their vertebrae pop.

Click. The next slide showed a seawall holding back dunes of sand. A cartoon character buried up to his nose in sand clung to the wall by his fingertips.

"It may seem ironic that an international symposium titled 'Worldwide Desertification of Arable Lands' should choose a lush sub-tropical state for its meeting place, but don't get too comfortable. My lecture this morning is about a place that was once as wet as Florida, which changed to arid wasteland like—" He snapped his fingers. "—that."

Porter chuckled. "Of course, that won't really happen to you in Florida. Rising sea levels from global warming are going to submerge your coastal lands long before then."

No one laughed.

Click. A map of Africa displayed.

"In a symposium about desertification, it is appropriate that we look at the world's largest desert, the Sahara, and surprising scientific findings about how it came to be. But let me make it clear that just because the Sahara was created by natural causes, does not mean every other desert was or is."

Dylan dug his laptop out of his backpack and turned it on, ready to take notes. This was a desert he was really interested in.

Porter pressed the clicker and glanced over his shoulder to make sure he was on the correct slide. A panorama of tan sand dunes stretched to the horizon beneath a pink sky—sunrise or sunset? Dylan couldn't tell.

"The Sahara covers a land area the size of the continental United States. It is also the hottest place on the surface of the Earth, a barren waste-land. The central desert receives less than two-and-a-half centimeters of rainfall a year. Until the late twentieth century, the Sahara was thought to have been the way it is now for at least three million years."

The next slide was a black-and-white photo of workers around a drilling rig. "That began to change in 1956, when the French discovered oil there. As they drilled exploratory wells across the Sahara, they found something they never expected, vast quantities of underground water. Where did that come from?"

Click. Porter glanced at the screen—the slide showed an oasis. "Sure, there have always been isolated oases, where enough fresh water seeped from a crack in the rocky surface to support a small populace and passing camel caravans, but they were few and far between. This was different. Wells, two hundred feet deep, tapped into enough water to irrigate large quantities of land. The question remained, if it has only rained a few centimeters a year for the last three million years, how did all that fresh water get down there?"

Another click, and a patchy view from outer space appeared. "Then in 1981, a NASA space shuttle scanned a forty-eight kilometer wide swath of the Sahara with a new type of ground-penetrating radar. It revealed a buried network of ancient waterways crisscrossing the desert."

Dylan nodded. These weren't new discoveries, but undoubtedly Porter was leading up to something.

Porter turned on a laser pointer and used its red dot to trace various areas of the image. "A colleague from the Kings College Geology department, Dr. Nick Drake, linked GPS coordinates to the NASA and other satellite images, and then traveled to North Africa to investigate those locations."

Repeatedly glancing between the PowerPoint and his laptop screen, Dylan recorded the GPS numbers that Porter indicated. But before he could finish, the slide changed to a man in his forties, pointing at a ribbon of shells embedded in an exposed cliff.

"Here, Dr. Drake found shells of millions of freshwater mollusks along what was once the shoreline of an ancient lake. Once he identified the land formations that delineated the lakeshore, he realized these lakes had been massive—hundreds of thousands of square kilometers. For comparison's sake, Lake Superior is about 82 thousand square kilometers. Drake dubbed these bodies of water mega-lakes."

Porter switched to a map of the Sahara on which had been drawn large irregular shaped green blobs. "Visiting other GPS positions from the satellite images, Professor Drake found evidence that mega-lakes had once existed all across the Sahara, in Chad, southern Libya, and Tunisia. He estimates that when filled with water, they would have covered ten percent of the Sahara. In contrast to the way it looks today, this Sahara would have been lush, green, and fertile, teeming with life."

Yes! He'd reviewed that book last night to double-check, and the author had never mentioned mega-lakes. Dylan waved his arm.

"Please hold your questions until the end of the lecture." Porter said. "Heretofore, the theories of how our ancestors left Africa were predicated on the notion that the Sahara was impossible to cross. But if, as evidence seems to indicate, the area that is now desert was once covered with numerous mega-lakes, interconnected by a system of rivers, they could have easily followed a green corridor all the way."

"Or used ships," Dylan blurted out.

"What's that, young man?"

"If you live on a mega-lake, you learn how to get around by ship," Dylan said quickly. "They could use those same skills to get around the Mediterranean."

"Not impossible, young man. But, again, please hold any discussion questions until—"

"Professor Porter, doesn't a water-covered Sahara support German researcher Michael Hübner's argument for placing Atlantis in northwest Africa?"

This was met with dead silence from the audience, except for a couple of snickers.

Porter's face turned crimson. "Who are you with, sir—the History Channel? You reporters are always trying to goad academics into making statements that could become headlines. Well, you won't find anyone here who believes Plato's stories are anything more than myths."

Dylan sunk down in his seat. "I-I'm not a reporter. I'm a doctoral student here, and my question was serious."

"Well, then, I pity you. A scholar who chases after lost cities is going to lose his credibility before he earns his PhD. Now, let us move on." Porter pressed his clicker. A graph of annual rainfall measurements displayed. The almost unwavering line varied little from year to year.

"With less than three centimeters of rainfall per annum, where did mega-lakes come from? It would require monsoon-like cycles to sustain lakes the size of these in an area too close to the equator to be fed by snowmelt."

Click. A video of a large sand dune filled the screen. Wind driven wisps of sand sailed into the sky from the dune's peak.

"For millennia upon millennia, winds swept across the Sahara's surface and deposited layers of its soil into the Atlantic Ocean."

Click. The image of a drill rig in the ocean filled the screen.

"Ocean geologists from Columbia University have published a scientific analysis of core samples extracted from the ocean floor off the coast of North Africa."

The next slide showed a man standing beside a deep-sea core sample that had been laid on its side and slit open to reveal strata of compacted sediment in various hues, like a roll of LifeSavers candy.

Porter again turned on the laser pointer and moved its red dot horizontally along the image of the core sample as he spoke. "These reddish sections were accumulated dust from the Sahara blown into the sea during its desert periods. The dark green and brown layers came from minerals that make up the normal seabed. They accumulated during periods when the Sahara had sufficient water to support groundcover to prevent the soil from blowing into the sea."

The slide changed to a close-up of the core. Porter shone the laser beam at the junction between the greenish-brown layer and the beginning of a bright red segment. "Each centimeter represents about two hundred years. The suddenness of the transition between these two layers shows us that a completely vegetated Sahara suddenly switched to one that was bone dry within just one or two centuries. The core samples prove that the Sahara regularly alternated from well-watered grasslands with mega-lakes to arid wasteland at 20,000 year intervals."

Porter's lecture continued for another forty-five minutes, with Dylan furiously taking notes. Dylan checked the time on his phone and saw Porter had run long. Darn. There'd be no time for questions.

The current slide displayed an aerial view encompassing the whole Sahara. "Dips in the desert floor provide geological evidence of monsoons. Where did these monsoons come from, and where did they go?"

Porter paused to take a sip of water. "The answer is, in wet cycles, monsoons shifted northward, watering the Sahara. Then suddenly the rain belt moves further south and doesn't return north for twenty millennia."

Click. Next was an artist's rendering of our solar system on the edge of the Milky Way. The laser pointer danced on the screen around the Earth. "I am sure everyone here is aware of what astronomers call obliquity of the elliptic, the degree of tilt of the Earth's rotational axis. This angle is not fixed. It varies due to planetary perturbations. A Parisian astrophysicist was able to compute that our axial tilt shifts in 20,000 year cycles—exactly matching the wet/dry cycles of the Sahara. Apparently, this slight fluctuation in our planet's obliquity is sufficient to alter the pattern of monsoons in Africa."

From his vantage point, Dylan saw Dr. Gujarat signal Dr. Porter with a slashing motion across his throat. Porter gave him a quick nod. "Of course, in our current climate crisis, we are the source of our own demise. But I think in the case of the Sahara, much larger forces—planetary forces—were at work."

Dr. Gujarat stepped from the wings, applauding. "Thank you very much, Dr. Porter." Gujarat turned to the audience. "I'm sorry we don't have time for questions, but you can talk with Dr. Porter in the lobby, or at this evening's reception."

Porter scooped up his papers, and Dylan sprang to his feet, heading toward him. Porter glanced in his direction and made for the exit. Dylan knew the professor saw him, but he'd hurried away as though he hadn't. He chased after him anyway.

"Dr. Porter, Dylan Clarke." He grabbed Porter's hand, uninvited, and shook it. "I think you're really onto something."

"Kind of you to say so. I've been studying deserts since you were in a pram."

That was kind of dismissive, even though probably true.

"I'd like to talk with you further," Dylan said. "Can I buy you a cup of coffee? Wait, you're English. Let me buy you a cup of tea."

"No thank you. One can't get a decent cup of tea in America. Your restaurants won't boil the water." Porter turned to move away.

Dylan turned with him.

"Sorry," Porter said, "I've got to find the audio-visual person and retrieve my USB stick."

"I'll show you where to go. I helped organize the conference."

Porter shrugged. "Your family Irish?"

Dylan recognized Porter's transparent attempt to lead the conversation away from Atlantis. "You mean because of my red hair?"

"No, your forename. I thought perhaps your parents named you after Dylan Thomas."

He shook his head. "More American Hippie. Bob Dylan."

"Of course."

Dylan led Porter to the A-V person, an informally dressed undergrad wearing a blue tee-shirt imprinted with an orange alligator head. The kid, obsessively tapping on his iPhone with both thumbs, paused long enough to hand Porter the USB, then went back to his phone.

They exited the conference area. Dylan followed Porter across the hotel lobby. "These mega-lakes you discovered . . . I know you're skeptical of Hübner's theory, but please hear me out."

Porter stopped. "First, I didn't discover the lakes. Nick Drake did. Second, I've never read anyone named Hübner, and I assure you, I'm well versed in the experts in my field."

"Michael Hübner, the German researcher? He organized geographical details, measurements, and other clues from Plato, then applied a series of mathematical formula to render coordinates that satisfied all the hierarchal constraints. He pinpointed the location of Atlantis on the Souss-Massa plain in Northwest Africa. His methods were not *that* different from those of your colleague, Nick Drake."

Porter paused. "Did you say earlier you were working on your doctorate?"

Dylan nodded. "As we say in America, ABD, All-But-Dissertation. I've finished all the coursework."

"Then let me give you some advice. Put Atlantis out of your mind. Strike the word from your vocabulary. If your thesis committee thinks you're chasing fairytales, they'll never grant your degree. Perhaps the philosophy department—they might tolerate it if you kept the focus on Plato."

"No, sir. My field is geophysics and climatology."

"Good. Then, the matter is settled. Atlantis has nothing to do with either." Porter headed for his room.

Dylan continued to walk beside him. "Please, hear me out, Professor. The only element Hübner couldn't explain was that his calculations positioned a seafaring civilization inland from the coast. But the work you've presented is the missing piece. Using interconnected waterways and mega-lakes, Atlantis would have had access to the ocean and even the whole of North Africa."

Porter shook his head. "You cannot make facts fit wild theories—or rather you can, with enough ingenuity. But you can fit those same facts to any number of theories, and Ockham's Razor exists for a reason. Do yourself a favor, attend Dr. Gujarat's session later today. He'll be discussing archeological sites showing humans lived in the Sahara when it was a lush and rich with game."

Dylan knew that. He'd proofread Dr. Gujarat's PowerPoint.

Porter held up a cautionary finger. "Evidence shows these were primitive hunter-gatherers, not some superhuman race with flying vehicles and submarines."

"You may be mistaking Hübner for some kook who claims Atlanteans arrived here in a UFO and seeded human civilization. He merely postulated a maritime kingdom at a location he arrived at through mathematical probability calculations."

Porter fished out his keycard and waved it at the sensor on his door. He pressed down on the handle and turned back to Dylan. "Listen to me. The most important thing I can tell you is, even mentioning Atlantis to a serious scholar will diminish your credibility and tarnish your academic reputation. Forget Atlantis."

"One more thing, professor."

"Yes?"

"Could I borrow your thumb drive?"

"May I ask why?"

"I'd like a copy of your presentation." He started to pull his laptop from his backpack. "It'll just take a second."

Porter gave him a grim look and shook his head. "I can't have my name associated with any foolish theories about Atlantis, and I fear that is exactly why you want it."

He wasn't wrong. "But I won't use your name—"

"Sorry. The answer is no." Porter stepped inside and closed the door behind him.

Chapter 3
Witnesses to the Last Rain

Dr. Gujarat's lecture was nearly over by the time Dylan showed up.

Oh, well, couldn't be helped—his stomach had won out. He'd missed breakfast and wasn't about to skip lunch, and the university didn't pay grad students enough to afford the Hilton Conference Center's restaurant, so he'd biked home, scarfed down a cheese sandwich, and grabbed a quick shower. After two sweaty bicycle rides, he needed that, and a clean shirt.

Dylan knocked on neighboring apartments until he found someone to jump start his car. Then, afraid it wouldn't start again, he drove it to an auto store. They tested the battery and told him what he expected—that the one that came with the car when he bought it seven years ago had finally expired. He needed a new one. What he didn't expect was how long it would take for them to install it.

The bright side was that the trip home had provided him an opportunity to fetch a map he wanted to show some of the scientists speaking at the conference.

On the screen, Dr. Gujarat had a photo of members of an archeology team standing at a dig site. On a tarp next to the hole were displayed an array of Stone Age tools and the jawbone of a small herbivore, perhaps a gazelle.

Dylan took the nearest seat and opened his laptop.

"These were discovered at a site not far from one of the mega-lakes Dr. Porter described this morning." Porter, sitting in the front row, nodded. "This particular lake would have stretched into what is modern-day Tunisia."

Now he really needed the GPS coordinates on Dr. Porter's slides.

The next slide showed a photo of—according to the caption on the slide —Egyptian geoarchaeologist Fekri Hassan, PhD. He hurriedly typed the name. Hassan looked like a kindly grandfather, with gray hair and charming mustache. His wire-rimmed glasses were tinted pale brown— probably necessary for the desert sun.

"Fanning out across the Sahara, scientists have excavated similar signs of man's presence on the shores of other mega-lakes," Gujarat said. "Human bones found in gravesites along the lakeshores range from 6,000 to 10,000 years old."

Although Dr. Gujarat didn't show those, Dylan understood the impact of this area being rich in biological life would have on our understanding of history and the development of mankind over the millennia.

His next slide featured circular arrangements of stone blocks with upright standing blocks. "This site in a Libyan desert valley is of a more recent settlement—radiocarbon dated to about seven thousand years ago. The stones in the circles were quarried from local bedrock and form the foundations of a group of houses in a settled farming community."

The slide changed to a shot of Dr. Hassan apparently at a higher altitude, standing at the mouth of a cave. "In hills above the settlement, Hassan found an important site that he believes pinpoints when this area last turned to desert. Before excavation, the cave was filled with sand almost as deep as he was tall. This was one indicator of how long the area had been dry because, according to Hassan, 'windblown sand cannot form when the desert is green.'"

Dylan pulled out his smartphone and googled Fekri Hassan. The man held degrees in both geology and anthropology, previously taught at Washington State University, acted as advisor to the Ministry of Culture of Egypt, and held the chair of Archaeology at the Institute of Archaeology and Department of Egyptology of University College London. Whew! Hassan was also the author of *Droughts, Food and Culture: Ecological Change and Food Security in Africa's Later Prehistory*. Dylan wondered why he wasn't speaking at the symposium. It seemed like he'd fit right in.

Gujarat was still talking. "Once he got inside the cave, he found animal droppings preserved by the drifted sand. These provided excellent material for radiocarbon dating and also allowed us to learn about the climate from the animal's diet. Exploring deeper into the cave, he found human handprints on the walls. He also discovered a cave drawing of a cloud with long wavy lines coming down, which he takes to mean rain." A slide showed a photo of the cave painting.

Dylan agreed. It looked like a kindergartener drew a rainstorm.

"Dr. Hassan believes this last great drying of the desert led to widespread migration. From different places in the desert, people migrated toward the Nile. Along its fertile valley, they reestablished their villages, and within a short time gave rise to the Egyptian civilization."

Dylan smiled. Ironically, the claim that the Egyptians had their origins from other more western civilizations was one of the 'crackpot theories' that scientists automatically dismissed.

"His conclusion is that, in this particular case, climate change stimulated one of the most spectacular civilizations in world history." Gujarat paused to chuckle. "Of course, as honorary president of the Egyptian

Cultural Heritage Organization, Hassan must be forgiven his partiality."

Gujarat concluded his presentation and answered a few questions, but Dylan had learned better than to ask his in front of an audience. The audience applauded, stood, and milled about, consulting their symposium schedules for the next event.

Dylan tucked his phone in his pocket, dropped the laptop in his backpack, and made a beeline for the stage where Gujarat and Porter were chatting.

"Professor Gujarat, I very much enjoyed your presentation."

Gujarat's eyes twinkled. "You missed most of it. I saw you come in at the end."

Dylan felt his face redden. "Car trouble. But from what I did hear, I certainly learned a lot about Dr. Hassan's discoveries. I wondered why he wasn't invited."

"Oh, of course we invited him, but he's supervising an excavation and didn't want to leave his work."

"Ah. Do you have a few minutes? I'd like to get your opinion on something. Dr. Porter, this will interest you as well."

Gujarat checked his watch and nodded. "Sure. The next session in this room doesn't start until three-thirty."

"Sorry, Gujarat," Porter said. "I'm afraid I can't stay."

Dylan frowned. "But Dr. Porter—"

"No. I've got to call London. Different time zone, you know."

"All right, Geoffrey, I'll see you at the reception," Gujarat said. "Dylan, let's sit over there." He led Dylan to a group of chairs haphazardly scattered along the wall near a table lined with bottles of local spring water.

Gujarat picked one up, twisted off the cap, and poured it into a hotel glass. He offered the glass to Dylan and poured another for himself. Gujarat deposited the empty bottles in a recycle bin.

When they were seated, Gujarat said, "So, Dylan, how is your dissertation coming? Any decision?"

"Still in the research phase."

Gujarat raised an eyebrow.

Dylan set his water on the seat of a nearby chair and unzipped his backpack. He hadn't spoken to Dr. Gujarat yet, since he wasn't sure what he might add to Hübner's research. But with the discovery of the megalakes, he now felt he had something to contribute to his field. Now was the time to present it. He removed an oversize sheet of copy paper that had been folded in half. "Are you familiar with this?"

He unfolded a Xeroxed map and handed it to Gujarat.

Gujarat accepted the Xerox and gave it a quick glance. "Yes. The map of Herodotus."

The ancient map, constructed from the writings of the first Greek historian, clearly showed familiar features, the boot-shape of Italy, the right-angle edge of southern Spain, the narrow gap of Gibraltar, labeled Pillars of Hercules. The Mediterranean, Caspian, and Atlantic seas were labeled. Misshaped continents represented Europe, Northern Africa, Central Eurasia, and Arabia. "Quite a good map for 430 BC," Dylan said.

Dylan pointed to the western part of North Africa where the Atlas Mountains lay. The land below the mountains, near the Atlantic coast, was labeled "Atlantis."

Gujarat handed it back to him. "This is only a copy of an ancient rendering of his map. No one has found the original. For all we know, it could have burned with the library at Alexandria."

"True," Dylan said. "But what's interesting is that everyone says Plato is the first to mention Atlantis, yet here it is on the map of a historian who had died by the time Plato was born."

The professor made a heavy sigh. "So, are you to become one of those who chase lost civilizations?"

"Didn't you just show us that Dr. Hassan discovered a lost settlement?"

Gujarat tugged his earlobe absentmindedly. "That's what archeologists hope for, but Fekri Hassan would be appalled if anyone thought he was implying this tiny village was Atlantis."

"No, of course it's not. Libya is too far east."

"I'm afraid you've missed the point. The importance of Hassan's discovery was that it dated the Sahara's most recent return to desert, documented in cave paintings by a generation that saw it happen."

"Yes, but his idea about them migrating to settle Egypt seems very likely."

"You'd have to take that up with him. I'm only reporting what he found, not arguing his case for him."

"You said these were farmers. The sudden shift from plentiful crop-supporting rainfall to scorching dunes in just a generation or two undoubtedly forced them to seek greener pastures elsewhere."

"Obviously, but these were Stone Age farmers, not some seafaring nation. I don't see what that has to do with Atlantis."

"It doesn't. I just find it interesting that Dr. Porter, and now you, both presented evidence of a North Africa covered with vast lakes. Meanwhile, the Greek father of history positions Atlantis on the western side of this same section of the African continent."

"What do you want me to tell you? I'm not into Atlantis. Porter and I are only presenting these findings on the Sahara to provide context to our current climate crisis. By identifying elements that can be attributed to natural cycles and removing them from the equation, what remains will be solely manmade causes. Those we can correct. All of this is science. But Atlantis? Atlantis is myth."

True. But so was Troy until Schliemann discovered it in the nineteenth century.

Chapter 4
A Nice Surprise

After parting ways with Dr. Gujarat, Dylan roamed the conference center and hotel lobby. There was a mixer for symposium attendees at six o'clock, and he didn't want to drive home only to turn around and come right back—gas cost money, too. He went into the hotel bar where he decided even the cheapest beer on tap was too pricey. Drinks would be free at the mixer. He went to check on his undergrads and then wandered around until six.

Once the reception started, Dylan mingled, carrying a cold beer with its label wrapped in a paper napkin. He kept an eye out for Dr. Porter, but the man was a no show. In the meantime, he tried to bring up the subject of the map of Herodotus to several people, but they'd either stare at him as if he'd sprouted six arms, or they suddenly spotted someone else they just *had* to see. Was this theory of an undiscovered kingdom as far out as that?

Then he bumped into an auburn-haired beauty. He turned to apologize at the same time she did, and—

Ohmygod!

"Holly?"

"Hello, Dylan."

He hadn't seen his ex-girlfriend in three years, and she looked better than ever. Better even than in this morning's dream.

They'd hooked up as undergrads the first night they'd met, which was how things used to happen back then. You'd meet at a party or club, and if the attraction was mutual, the next thing you knew, the two of you were doing a horizontal tango.

But they'd barely finished making love before their post-coital pillow talk turned to science and he knew he was in bed with a certified genius. She knew things about the mechanisms that drove the climate that he was only just getting hints of. And she talked about them with passion and insight. It was like being thrown into a seminar class on a favorite subject with a brilliant professor. They had talked for hours. And the next morning, she told him that she'd never been with a man who was attracted to her mind as much as her body. Most guys were so intimidated as soon as she opened her mouth that she never saw them again.

That held true for the balance of their relationship—they'd moved in together after a month. On any given day, she was ten times smarter than he was, and he genuinely loved her for it. He learned from her and was happy to do it. It was as if behind Holly's eyes were bright LEDs that illuminated answers where he'd only seen raw data. She made him a better scientist, and she said his support gave her the courage to be open about her passion.

It lasted two years. Then came grad school and Holly won a fellowship at the Godwin Laboratory, Cambridge, an English university he couldn't dream of getting into. They mutually agreed there was no practical way to maintain their relationship across an ocean and parted as friends. He had regretted it ever since.

And now, three years later, she was standing in front of him with a shiny new prefix on her nametag: *Dr.* Holly Johnson. Naturally. He decided to skip mentioning Herodotus.

He reached out to shake her hand, because that's what everyone at the conference was doing. But before he could, she leaned over and gave him a peck on the cheek. "Forget to shave?"

He swallowed hard. "Only today."

Holly wore glasses, usually atop her head like a hairband. She slipped them from her hair and put them on. "You look well, Dylan."

"I am well. And you look . . . fantastic."

She straightened his tie. "You kept the tie I gave you."

"Save it for special occasions." He pointed to her name tag. "Congratulations. I see you finished your doctorate."

"Yeah, but I'm working on another one. Applied statistics, this time."

Of course she would be. He knew she hadn't said it to brag, she wasn't a bragger. She was just filling him in on her life. "Is that why you're back at UF?" A faint hope wavered in his heart.

She cocked her head. "No. I'm presenting at the symposium. Didn't you know?"

How had he missed that? He looked into his memory and recalled the events listed in the symposium program. He'd re-read it so many times he could recite it by rote. There she was: Thursday, 3:00 p.m. in the Azalea Room—Dr. H. Johnson. He'd failed to make the connection.

"I hope you'll be there," Holly was saying.

"I wouldn't miss it." The thought came unbidden. Did that mean a nocturnal reunion afterward?

He snapped his attention back to their conversation. "I'll be in the front row." His eyes wandered her body with the familiarity of an old boyfriend. "You're very suntanned. You didn't get that in England."

She laughed. "No, I've been working on a project in North Africa."

Africa? Maybe he'd show her the map of Herodotus, after all. "That's someplace I'm interested in, too. Do you want to get out of here? I'm still living in our old apartment. We can be there in ten minutes."

She laid her hand on his in a way that he perceived as seductive, but her words were saying the opposite. "No. As much as I'd like to, we can't go there."

Damn. "But I have something you'll want to see."

Holly's eyes twinkled. "I've seen it, and I'll want to again, but not tonight. I have to practice my presentation. I don't want to be fumbling with my slides like Geoffrey Porter did."

His face must have revealed his disappointment, for she touched her cool, slender fingers to his cheek. "Don't fret. I'll be here all week. Just let me get through tomorrow and then ask me again."

Chapter 5
The Disappearing Sea

The next afternoon, Dylan arrived early for Holly's presentation and sat in the front row. Running into her at the reception had resurfaced an awful lot of stuff. Emotions he'd lacked the maturity to express a few years ago now bubbled up like the clear Florida springs projected on the screen behind her.

She stepped to the podium and tapped the microphone. "Before we get to the main topic of my presentation, I want to get something off my chest." Holly pointed to the tables along the perimeter of the room, covered with half-liter plastic bottles of water. "I grew up in a small town just north of Gainesville that is known for numerous freshwater springs. My friends and I swam and tubed in their cool, constant seventy-two-degree waters."

Dylan thought about the many hot summer days he and Holly had floated on inner tubes down the Ichetucknee River and swum at Ginnie springs.

"A company that owns the land around Ginnie Springs has a permit allowing it to take out nearly 1.2 million gallons of water a day. Companies owned by Nestlé, Coca-Cola, and many others package it in individual plastic bottles, just like those on the tables at the back of this room. Four years ago, state water managers determined that the flow in the Santa Fe

River and nearby springs had declined below a level that's sustainable. It strikes me as ironic that a symposium on desertification is sitting around sipping Florida's natural habitat into oblivion. While we're figuring out what to do in Africa and elsewhere, maybe we ought to stop buying bottled water and allow Florida's aquifer to recover."

Dylan clapped loudly, and she smiled at him. A few others caught on, and she received a smattering of applause from the audience.

"I'm not suggesting that Florida is going to turn into the Sahara or even the Aral Sea, but they are cautionary tales from which we should learn. So, speaking of the Aral Sea. . ."

The photo of beautiful teal springs he and Holly had swum in was replaced by a satellite image of brown earth with two lopsided, dark blue ponds.

"The Aral Sea, which spans the borders of Kazakhstan and Uzbekistan, is an endorheic basin, fed by an inflow from the Amu Darya and Syr Darya rivers. Without an outflow to any ocean, water which kept it filled for millennia should have maintained its levels."

The next slide showed an aerial view of a large, dark sea of water.

"This is what the Aral looked like in 1989." Holly changed the slide to one of a gray-brown desert with a long thin puddle on the left and a few small connected puddles at the top. "This was the Aral in 2014."

Dear God. He had no idea this was happening. He turned to his neighbors, but they seemed to have seen the images before.

"The shrinking of what was at one time the fourth largest lake on earth has been called 'one of the planet' s worst environmental disasters.'"

Holly's next slide showed a poorly maintained irrigation canal and a desiccated cotton plant that looked to be nothing more than a brown stalk with a few cotton balls clinging precariously.

"Following World War II, irrigation canals proliferated in an attempt to grow cotton, melons, and rice by diverting water from the Aral. But these worked no better than any of Stalin's centrally planned agricultural projects. The canals were poorly constructed and lost up to seventy-five percent of the water to leakage and evaporation. In the early sixties, Soviets decided to divert water from the rivers that sustained the lake as well, and the Aral began to shrink. Its water level was dropping twenty centimeters a year. By 1970, that figure had tripled to sixty centimeters a year. In the eighties, that loss zoomed to ninety centimeters per year. By 1998, the sea's surface area had shrunk by sixty percent and its volume by eighty percent."

The image of a rusting fishing trawler lying on the dry lake basin was next.

"Wasteful agricultural irrigation brought with it pesticide and fertilizer runoff, which created severe pollution. The water loss increased the lake's salinity, which devastated the area's fishing industry. By 2007, the Southern Aral was less than ten percent of its original size and most of the natural flora and fauna had died out. By 2014, the eastern basin had completely dried up and is now known as the Aralkum Desert."

A satellite image credited to NASA appeared on screen with the Aralkum Desert highlighted.

"While the Sahara may have been caused by planetary shift, the Aralkum is proof positive of man's destructive capability. We have witnessed in just two generations the transformation of a vast body of water into a desert wasteland."

There was stunned silence in the audience. It wasn't that these scientists had not already known of the Aral—now that he thought about it, Dylan remembered reading about it as well. But Holly's pictures and lecture had so clearly brought home what manmade climate change truly looked like. Dylan felt proud of the job she had done, though irrationally, as he'd had nothing to do with her presentation and she hadn't even been his girlfriend for years. He caught her eye as she scanned her audience and beamed at her. She smiled back and pressed the clicker for the next slide.

A small crew of hardhats was working on a tall drilling rig.

"Now, let us turn to the Sahara," Holly said. "Geoffrey Porter showed us in his presentation that there are vast reserves of groundwater under the Sahara. Helen Bonsor from the British Geological Survey and University College London believes the greatest groundwater storage is in northern Africa, in large sedimentary basins in Libya, Algeria, and Chad."

A map of North Africa appeared on the screen.

"Ground-penetrating radar reveals aquifers throughout the region. The temptation to turn the Sahara green with farms and agriculture seems irresistible. In fact, plans are underway to bore two hundred wells there. But have we learned nothing from the Aral?"

Acres of green fields being cultivated by a score of tractors at some a large-scale agriculture operation replaced the image of the map.

"Yes, vast reserves of water have been discovered under a burning, searing, thirsty land. But this is prehistoric water that seeped into the sediment layers from monsoons five thousand years ago. Nothing is replenishing those reserves until the Earth's axis shifts again—fifteen thousand years from now."

The next slide showed a group of African men and women gathered around a community well.

"Widespread drilling for large-scale agribusiness is a disaster in the making. It could quickly deplete the reservoirs and create other unforeseen consequences. But . . . a paper Dr. Bonsor co-authored suggests that small-scale extraction using hand pumps would be more sustainable for a much longer term than large-scale drilling projects."

A new slide showed a map of identified aquifers beneath the Sahara.

"The UK study found sufficient groundwater under North Africa to support low yielding water supplies for drinking and community irrigation. This will have a profound impact on some of the world's poorest people, making them less vulnerable to drought and the impact of climate change."

Holly smiled at her audience. "Now, if I could only convince Nestlé to do the same in Florida." This time, her audience laughed.

Afterwards, Dylan was the first to reach her. "Wonderful presentation, Holly. Can I take you to dinner tonight?" He didn't have that much in the bank, especially after springing for a battery, but he'd splurge for her.

Her eyes danced, telegraphing her delight. "I'd love that. Sorry that I blew you off last night, but I had to practice." She interlaced her fingers with his. "That's over now. Yes, let's get out of here."

"Are you hungry? It's pretty early for dinner."

"Oh, we don't have to eat yet. I'm tired of being cooped up in lectures from morning to night, aren't you? Let's drive over to Lake Alice and follow the boardwalk around the lake."

They held hands as they walked to his car. It felt like old times.

Chapter 6
Not Quite the Night He Hoped

Dylan drove Holly to a charming Italian restaurant less than a mile from the hotel. It was the last building in a strip mall, but inside, the ambiance made up for its rather drab commercial location. Dark wooden furniture and white linen napkins classed the place up a bit. A solo guitarist in the corner strummed jazz chords. Dylan asked the hostess for a quiet table away from the music. He wanted nothing to distract them. They hadn't been out together in three years and had a lot of ground to cover.

The hostess led them to a table in the back, and Dylan pulled out Holly's chair for her.

"My, my," she said. "You're making an effort."

He grinned like it was their first date. "The effort's worth making."

The hostess handed them menus and lit the candle in the red glass holder on the table. Its rosy glow tinted Holly's face. She slipped her glasses from atop her hair, put them on, and studied the menu.

A dark-haired waitress wearing black slacks and a crisp white blouse arrived with two glasses of ice water, and asked for their drink orders. Dylan ordered a carafe of the house Chianti. She disappeared for a moment, then returned with it, and filled their glasses. She set the carafe on the table next to him. "Are you ready to order?"

Dylan shook his head. "Give us a few minutes."

He was tempted to order the garlic rolls, but that might put the kibosh on his chances for a romantic ending to the evening.

Holly looked up from her menu. "How about some garlic rolls?"

"Sure." If they both ate garlic, neither would be offended. "Did you decide what you want for your entrée?"

"Eggplant Parmigiana."

He chose spaghetti—cheapest thing on the menu.

"It was nice to see Lake Alice again," Holly said. "Thanks for taking me there."

He loosened his damp shirt. "You don't mind ninety-five percent humidity?"

"After half a year in the desert, lush, green, and wet is a welcome change."

"But isn't it a dry heat?"

She laughed. "So is my oven."

He thought he could bear the heat if they were working there together. After hearing about the ancient mega-lakes, he had decided he needed to get to Africa somehow, anyway. He wasn't sure he could convince Professor Gujarat there was a dissertation topic in Atlantis, but he stood a much better chance if he actually went there and surveyed the evidence himself. How much better would it be to go there with a woman he loved?

After dinner, they split a tiramisu, and then drove back to his apartment.

"You haven't changed a thing," Holly said when she entered.

"No reason to. I liked the way we had it when you left." He walked to the desk and picked up a folder of papers. "I did buy a new computer, though."

"Me, too."

He pointed to the couch. "You don't have to stand. Make yourself at home."

Holly sat on the same side of the couch where she always had. Her choice brought a wave of nostalgia, and he took his place next to her.

She glanced at the folder. "What's that?"

"Something about Africa I want you to read." He handed her a dog-eared document printed from his computer: *New Evidence for a Large Prehistoric Settlement in a Caldera-Like Geomorphological Structure in Southwest Morocco* by Michael Hübner and Sebastian Hübner.

He gave her a minute to read it over. "Did you visit this site while you were in Africa?" he asked in a voice tinged with hope.

She shook her head. "Never got to Morocco. Our NGO was based in Egypt. I did get to Libya once."

"NGO?"

"Non-Governmental Organization. It's what most foreign governments call non-profits that do some sort of social or humanitarian project in their counties. A few NGOs deal with political issues, human rights, and such—but most are nonprofits just there to give people some help. Ours was there to provide outlying villages with the capacity for clean water."

He tried not to look disappointed. It would have been a different conversation if she'd actually been there. "You might like Hübner's paper.

He used computer algorithms to identify a site southeast of Agadir, Morocco. When he checked Google Earth, he spotted the Richat, or Eye of the Sahara, exactly where his calculations led. It was a caldera-like structure with unique characteristics: a central hill, surround by concentric rings that appeared to be dry riverbeds, and a deep crevice that extended out to the Atlantic Ocean."

She thumbed the fifty-page report. "What was he looking for? I mean, what parameters did he put into his algorithms? Where did he get them?"

"Earlier reports of the civilization." Dylan cleared his throat. "Michael Hübner went there and found not only the specific geomorphological formations he was looking for, but the ruins of ancient buildings built from white, red, and black stones."

She glanced again at the title of the paper. "Interesting approach to discovering previously unknown archeological sites. Of course, satellites have changed our whole method of searching."

Dylan nodded. "They have, but with millions of satellite photos to sort through, it helps if you know where to look. That's where Hübner's algorithms came into play."

"So . . . I noticed you dodged the question about his source data?"

He hesitated. But if he couldn't trust her with this . . . "Plato."

Holly's mouth dropped open. "Plato?"

Dylan pointed to a stack of books on his desk. "Specifically, *Timaeus* and *Critias*. The dialogues are filled with precise numbers and measurements. Exactly what computers work with best."

"Oh, don't tell me this Hübner was searching for—"

"Atlantis, yes. And he found it."

Holly handed him the report with a laugh. "You really had me going there for a moment."

He pushed it back into her hands. "This isn't a joke, Holly. Just read it."

She shrugged. "Give me a minute." She skimmed a few pages, read the conclusions thoroughly, glanced at the indices, and looked up. "Okay, he's discovered an ancient settlement built on a hill in the center of up-raised geological formation surrounded by annular troughs. That could just be a caldera of some ancient volcano. Earth is covered with them."

"Not with a hill in the center of it." He took the paper from her, flipped to the Introduction, and handed it back. "He says here, 'The geological origin of this structure appears to be an anticline.' And a sentence later, 'No evidence of volcanism has been found in this particular area.'"

"That doesn't make it Atlantis, just a stone age settlement. Besides, it's too far from the ocean. Atlantis was an island."

"Ah, this is where things get interesting." Dylan retrieved an aerial photo from his folder and handed it to her. "Plato said Atlantis was 50 stades from the sea. That's about 12 kilometers." He drew his finger along a crevice connecting the Eye of the Sahara to the Atlantic. "Also, to describe the landmass of Atlantis, Plato uses the word *nesos*, which has five meanings in ancient Greek. Island is only one, but it can also mean a peninsula, or even an area within a continent surrounded by lakes. Nesos could describe Michigan, for example."

"You've been studying ancient Greek?"

"Not to speak it, but I read that during my research."

His voice rose in pitch, something he'd never been able to control. "But there's more! Every measurement Plato gave matches the dimensions of this formation." He handed her a topographical map of the area. "Plato said Atlantis was sheltered on two sides by mountains." He pointed to a mountain range on the map north of the Richat. "Can you read what it says?"

"Atlas Mountains."

"Exactly! And do you know the name of the first king of Atlantis?"

Holly shrugged. "Why would I?"

"Atlas."

Holly didn't say anything. This wasn't going the way he expected. Time for the big gun. He pulled out his copy of Herodotus' map. "Okay, forget Plato for a moment. Here is a map of the known world based on the writings of the first Greek historian. He died when Plato was only a year old, so his work precedes anything written by Plato. Now, look on his map along the coast of what is today, Morocco. The name he writes for that country is *Atlantis*."

Holly looked sad. "Dylan, is this really what you've been doing since I left?"

He handed her his whole folder. "Don't you see this is important? Look at the evidence I've compiled."

She leafed through the pages. "Tell me this isn't research for your doctorate."

He sensed a hint of tension in the room that wasn't present earlier. "I'd like it to be, but I'm not certain I can get Dr. Gujarat to agree. So I haven't started my dissertation yet. I'm thinking of taking a year off."

She tapped the papers. "Well, forget this business if you ever want a doctorate. Your committee will never accept it."

He never should have brought up Atlantis. His mind scrambled for a way to rekindle the spark that earlier had danced between them. Dylan took the folder from her and casually tossed on the floor. He took her hands in his and gazed deeply into her eyes, trying to reconnect, trying to reawaken the romance.

Come on, Holly, feel what I'm feeling.

Her reaction wasn't the one he anticipated. Holly's eyes darted toward the kitchen doorway, where their atomic clock always hung. It wasn't there. That clock displayed the temperatures indoor and out, but constantly lost signal with the outside sensor, so he'd moved it. He'd found a sketch she'd made of primitive canoes discovered under Newnans Lake, had it framed, and put it where the clock had been. And now she was noticing it. Would that bring back the magic?

She reached into his shirt pocket, pulled out his cell phone, and touched the power button. "Goodness. The time. You better take me back to the hotel. I have an early class."

So much for the magic. Was he wrong in thinking—

Wait! Class? "Are you back at UF?"

She stood and picked up her purse. "No, just for tomorrow. I promised Dr. Gujarat I'd guest lecture his morning geomorphology class."

"Oh." He could kick himself for wasting precious time talking about Atlantis when it could have been better spent hooking up. "Can I see you again?"

She pulled him close and gave him a lingering kiss. "I'll be here all week."

His heart raced. "Tomorrow night?"

She smiled. "Sure."

Chapter 7
The Contract

The next evening, Dylan kept his mouth shut about Atlantis, and Holly proved to be as happy to renew their physical relationship as he was. They hurriedly pulled off each other's clothes, tossed them aside, and fell into bed. Then they slowed. Caressing and kissing awakened something deeper than carnal urges. A steep nostalgia engulfed him as Holly responded in familiar ways that pleasured them both.

Smiling, fulfilled, she turned on her side, rested her damp thigh on his leg and her head on his chest. He inhaled the scent of her shampoo and kissed the top of her head. She reached for his hand, kissed his fingertips, and pulled his arm around her. It was perfect.

And he had already taken steps to make it more perfect.

Earlier that afternoon, he'd attended a lecture about an NGO-sponsored project to provide shallow wells and hand pumps to rural North Africa. It was the organization where Holly worked. He'd gone expecting to see her there, but she wasn't. For most of the presentation, he'd fantasized about traveling around North Africa with her, helping poor villagers find a source of clean water. Lying in bed, deep in afterglow, feeling her breath move the hairs on his chest, it seemed that was his destined course to follow.

"A penny for your thoughts," Holly said.

"When you go back to Africa, why don't we go together?"

She rolled off him and up on one elbow. "You're kidding."

"No. I heard a presentation from your NGO this afternoon, and they're recruiting more fieldworkers."

She sat up and pulled the sheet over her breasts. "What about your degree?"

"I'm thinking of taking a sabbatical."

She laughed. "Oh. I thought you were serious."

"I am serious."

"No, a sabbatical is what you take after you've taught twenty years. When you're ABD, what you're taking is called a mistake."

Dylan shrugged. "Call it a gap year, then. I'm ready to go with you."

Holly gave him a tiny kiss. "That's sweet, but it seems a little hasty."

"No. A lot of things are coming together. Things I've been thinking about for some time."

"You're crazy. We meet up after three years, have sex once, and you want to drop out and follow me?"

"It was very good sex."

"I agree, but not that good."

He sat up next to her. "It may seem sudden, I know, but I've always loved you. I made the mistake of my life by not going to England with you. Now's our second chance. We can be together while doing something good for the people there."

She shook her head. "Dylan, this idea is wrong on so many levels. You need to stay here and finish your dissertation. Otherwise, you're stuck with a measly masters and a lot of student-loan debt. Besides, I've got my own degree to work on." She stood and picked up her bra.

Once again, that didn't go the way he'd imagined.

"Holly." He pulled her back into bed. "Spend the night."

"Well, I intended to, until you brought all that up."

"Let's not argue." He pulled her close and kissed her for all it was worth. She tossed her bra on the floor.

A half hour later, she lay panting. "Whew. Sex is good, but make-up sex is the best."

He wasn't about to disagree.

They snuggled, drifting into a satisfied sleep.

In the morning, he eased out of bed without waking her, started the coffeemaker, and took a shower.

Holly slid open the shower door, stepped in, and kissed him on the back of his neck. "Good morning, love."

He spun around, embraced her, and pivoted so she was under the falling water.

While they were dressing, his phone started playing "Afterglow." He swiped the phone screen to silence it.

Holly's eyes met his. "You still have that song as your alarm?"

"Yeah, I guess I do." He glanced away. "You used to like it."

"I think it used to mean something different to us."

After a light breakfast, he drove her to the hotel, and they parted ways. It was the last day of the symposium and, as a UF staffer, he had to help with the takedown. He'd planned to see her again before she left for the airport, but his morning got busy and by the time he got a break she'd checked out.

Dylan thought about Holly throughout the day. He also thought about Atlantis. Opposition or no, he still wasn't ready to let it go. It was too significant. No matter where they were stationed in North Africa, it would only be a short hop to Morocco. She'd appreciate the romance of Casablanca and they'd take a Land Rover out to the Eye of the Sahara. The discovery would be theirs together.

On the spur of the moment, he hunted up the information table for the African well project, intending to sign up. But the table was bare of signage or literature. Dylan turned to a woman at the next table. "Do you know if these folks are coming back?"

"No. He left already. I think they filled all the positions they had open."

Dylan melodramatically clutched his heart. "Say it isn't so."

She gave him a practiced smile. "It isn't so."

"Really?"

"No. Or maybe. Here, have a free pen. Take a handful. I don't want to carry them home on the plane." She slipped a half dozen ballpoints in his shirt pocket.

"Uh. Thanks." Dylan wanted to kick himself for not signing up sooner. Apparently, Holly's group was more popular that he'd anticipated.

Later, he had to take the departmental equipment they'd used at the symposium to Dr. Gujarat's lab. It took several trips. He couldn't shake the fantasy of Holly and him working together in Africa. On his final trip, he decided to try one more thing. If he couldn't get into the program now, maybe he could get on a wait list.

At the hotel, he asked at the registration desk for the NGO rep's room number but was told he had left. Well, he'd heard it from two different sources. It must be true. He'd check their website as soon as he got home, call some 800 number, and try to finagle a job. Use Holly's name if he had to.

With a sigh, he headed to the parking lot and had almost reached the hotel's sliding glass doors when he spotted the NGO rep sitting in the lobby with his luggage. "Oh, hello. I was looking for you. I'm Dylan Clarke."

The man stood and shook his hand. "Robert Lansing. Call me Bob."

"I attended your session and wanted to sign up to work with your organization in Africa. But I guess you're all filled up."

"Really? Where'd you get that idea?"

"The woman at the table next to yours."

"She was mistaken. No one wanted to volunteer. I thought this trip was going to be for nothing."

"Well, I want to go. Can we do the paperwork now?"

"We don't have to. Just give me your info and my office can send you the contract and discuss the details over the phone."

Dylan shook his head. He wouldn't pass up the chance to surprise Holly. "If you have the necessary paperwork with you, I'd like to get started as soon as possible."

Bob glanced at his watch. "I have a five o'clock flight. I'm waiting for the airport shuttle."

"Surely signing the contract won't take long." He really wanted to get to Africa in time to be assigned to Holly's team.

"Signing? No. But the management in Cairo are sticklers about me explaining the commitment before you sign."

"My car is right outside. I'll drive you to the airport, and you can explain on the way."

Chapter 8
Egypt

The jet's wheels touched the hot tarmac as the engines reversed thrust and the pilot applied the brakes. The plane taxied to a gate and waited while the jetway slowly extended to its door. "Egypt Air is pleased to welcome you to Cairo," said a voice over the intercom, followed by some spritely, Middle Eastern Muzak.

The jetway was an oven, followed by an arctic blast of air conditioning in the terminal building. Dylan collected his suitcase from the carousal, then passed through immigration and customs.

"Mr. Clark-ee?" A pretty woman wearing a peach-colored hijab waved to him from behind a red line and a sign that said "No Re-entry" in several languages. Except for the headscarf, she was dressed like a westerner—jeans, sneakers, and a tee shirt that read: "Water is Life." The NGO's motto. She had almond-shaped brown eyes, an oval face, and a charming smile. "Mr. Clark-ee!"

"Just Clarke. The 'e' is silent."

Her smile turned to chagrin.

He stuck out his hand. "But please, call me Dylan. I'm happy to meet you."

She shook his hand. "Asenath Kamel."

"Ah, I hoped Dr. Johnson would come."

Her smile widened, and dimples appeared. "I'll be your liaison while you're here. Is that all the luggage you have?"

"Yes."

"Good, you paid attention to the recommendation to travel light. I'll bet you're exhausted. What was your flight, about twenty-five hours?"

Dylan yawned. "Thirty-one. I had a six-hour layover in Frankfurt."

"Ach, terrible. I have a car. Let's get you settled." She spoke excellent English, albeit with a slight British accent. Perhaps she'd attended the same university where Holly had done her doctorate.

Outside, the temperature surprised him. It didn't feel that different from Gainesville, except drier. She opened the doors of the car to let the heat escape while he put his suitcase in the trunk. When the interior was less oven-like, he got into the front seat.

She started the engine, set the A/C on high, and pulled out when there was a break in the traffic. "We have a guest house we always use. They bill the foundation directly, so if they ask, don't pay them anything."

They hadn't driven for very long before she wheeled into the driveway of a yellow two-story building. He retrieved his suitcase, and she accompanied him inside. She spoke to a woman in what he assumed was Arabic. The woman handed her a key, and Asenath took him to his room. It was . . . nice. A microwave sat on a counter next to a sink. A mini-refrigerator was tucked beneath the counter. There were two beds. He threw his suitcase on one of them and yawned. "Thank you for picking me up at the airport."

Asenath turned on the air conditioner. "Catch up on your sleep. The guest house serves breakfast from six until nine, but don't worry if you miss it. I'll take you out." She laid a card on the counter. "The office is closed tomorrow. Call my mobile when you wake up. We'll grab a bite and do some tourist things." She dropped the room key beside her card. "I'm going now. Welcome to Egypt. See you tomorrow."

The door closed behind her. He hoped he'd see Holly tomorrow—unless she was already in the field. He should have asked. Maybe he should have asked before he left, but he was hoping to surprise her, and she'd seemed pretty eager to talk him out of it earlier.

He picked up Asenath's card, looked at it. No. He was too tired. Dylan laid it back on the counter, stripped, took a shower, and fell into bed.

At 4:30 in the morning, speakers in the streets around the guest house began to blare in Arabic. It certainly wasn't Taylor Swift. Dylan struggled awake, trying to make sense of it, but couldn't, so he pulled the pillow over his head and tried to go back to sleep. After a few more repetitions, the noise ended. He pulled the pillow off his head and drifted off again.

He was next awakened by a loud knocking on his door. "Just a minute." He got up, then realized he was naked. A robe hung on a hook in the bathroom. He put it on, tied the sash, and cracked open the door. It was Asenath.

"You didn't call."

"I didn't wake up. Come on in."

She stepped in, leaving the door ajar. "I'd guessed you overslept. The quickest cure for jet lag is to eat at regular mealtimes in the local time zone. It resets our circadian rhythms. I'll wait outside while you get dressed." She left and closed the door behind her.

He threw on pants, a shirt, and Skechers without socks, his typical Florida hot-weather gear. They met in the lobby. Today she wore a cranberry-colored hijab and a tee shirt silkscreened with the album cover of *Damn the Torpedoes*. Dylan pointed to her chest. "They're from Gainesville, you know?"

"Who?"

"Tom Petty and the Heartbreakers."

"Really? Did you know them?"

"Before my time. But he's a Gainesville hero."

They walked to a café for lunch. He desperately needed coffee, but what he got was thick and black, and the bottom of his cup was full of grounds. Oh, well, any port in a storm—he drank two cups.

"How did you sleep?"

"Fine, until someone with a loudspeaker woke me up before dawn."

"Oh, the call to prayer. Did no one tell you about that?"

He shook his head.

"It's a Muslim tradition, pray five times a day. The first is at dawn."

He winced. "Something to look forward to."

"Today I thought I'd show you Wadi Al-Hitan. It's a national park about 150 kilometers from here. You can see the pyramids as we drive by, but we'd have to book a tour to get inside them, and it's too late to do that. We'll save them for another day."

"That sounds nice, thank you. Do you know if I'm being assigned to the same place Holly Johnson is working? I put that request on my paper-work."

"Dr. Johnson? I know her well. She worked for us last year. I understood she went back to the U.S."

"She did. But I met her there and got the impression she was coming back here to work."

"Definitely not. My job is to coordinate foreign staff for all our North Africa projects. Dr. Johnson resigned last month and left to earn an advanced degree."

Shit! She'd told him then she was working on a second doctorate, and she sure couldn't do that from the North African desert. What a bonehead he'd been.

"Are you finished?" Asenath said. "We better get on the road."

"Yeah." He was finished all right.

Chapter 9
Whales in the Desert

Asenath Kamel paid the tab for lunch. "Cheer up, it's just a little jet lag. Wadi Al-Hitan is going to—I believe the American expression is—blow your mind."

Dylan numbly followed Asenath to her car. He was stuck here and Holly was . . . who knew where? Now what was he supposed to do?

Well, he could still visit the site in Morocco. He might as well pursue Atlantis while he had a chance.

Asenath kept up a steady narration for the entire two-hour drive. "Contrary to common belief, sand dunes cover only fifteen percent of the Sahara, while seventy percent of it is gravel plains."

Dylan stared at the landscape and nodded absentmindedly. He'd known that from his geology course at UF. The remaining fifteen percent were stone plateaus, salt flats, and wadis. But as long as she was playing tour guide, he didn't have to engage in conversation.

What a fool he was.

She turned into the Wadi Al-Hitan Park and turned off the car. "You're allowed to drive into the park if you have a four-by-four, but since we don't, we'll leave the car here. There's a guided tour with a paleontologist

—that's better than driving ourselves, anyway. He'll take us right to the fossils."

Dylan needed to find out what happened to Holly. When she'd moved to the UK three years ago, she'd switched her phone plan to an international one. He still had her number and should be able to text her wherever she was. He found her contact info and typed: "Where are you? What are you doing?"

Asenath opened the glove box and pulled out a bottle of sunscreen. "Put this on. With your complexion, you'll burn in two minutes."

He slipped his phone into his pocket, and she squeezed white goop into his palm. Dylan rubbed his hands together and spread the sunscreen over his face, neck, and arms.

"When we get back to Cairo, we need to buy you a hat."

They got out of the car and walked over to a broad-faced man wearing a wide-brimmed hat and a khaki shirt who was talking to a small group of tourists. He welcomed them and the group set off at a leisurely pace.

Dylan still had sunscreen on his hands. He wiped them on his pants and checked his phone to see if Holly had replied. The screen displayed: *No signal. Message not sent.* Shit!

"This afternoon you will see the most important whale fossil discovery in history," the guide said.

Wait. Whale fossils?

"Protected in this World Heritage site," the guide said, "are over 1500 skeletons of excellent quality. Paleontologists have identified fossils from at least four species of whales, and several other marine animals." The guide gestured toward the surrounding wind-worn rocks. "The geology of the area indicates these are from the late to middle Eocene era.

Especially unique to Wadi Al-Hitan is the evidence it provides of the evolution of the whales from land animals to life at sea."

The guide led them up a gravel incline alongside an intact skeleton that Dylan estimated must be sixty-five feet long. "This specimen is a basilosaurus, a primitive whale. Of particular interest is the presence of these two hind limbs, not found in modern whales. Note the absence of an articulation with the sacral vertebrae. It means they were probably not used for locomotion, but possibly served as claspers during mating."

Whales in the desert. The middle Eocene era, the guide had said? So about 40 million years ago, give or take.

They climbed further and stood next to a skull full of sharp teeth. "This fellow was a carnivore, probably the top ocean predator of his period. To one of these, a great white shark would have made a nice hors d'oeuvre." He laughed at his own joke. "Of course, they didn't live during the same era."

Dylan looked around. They were above the valley by now. He pulled out his phone and held it toward the sky, turning slowly in a circle. Nothing.

"You may as well give up," Asenath said. "The nearest cell tower is in Faiyum, a good fifteen kilometers away."

He frowned.

"Give me your phone. I'll take your picture."

A tourist next to her said, "No, give it to me and I'll take the two of you together."

Dylan handed over his phone and stood with Asenath next to the whale's skull.

The others got their phones out and snapped selfies with the skeleton.

The guide returned to his spiel. "Notice that unlike modern toothed whales, this species has molars and canines. He or she could chew their food. Today's cetaceans can't do that and must swallow their food whole."

Dylan wasn't really interested in prehistoric animals. His field was geophysics and climatology, and his interest was Atlantis, which came millions of years later. So what was he doing in Egypt? Digging wells with Holly? Apparently not.

Since he already had his phone out, he took a long shot of the whale skeleton and a few close-ups of the toothy head.

The guide gently nudged him aside. "The forehead doesn't appear to have had room for the adipose tissue mass found in modern toothed whales and dolphins, thus it probably lacked echolocation capability." He turned the group around and directed them back down into the valley. "The next specimen is a smaller cousin, the dorudon."

"But how did all these whales get here?" one of the tourists asked.

Dylan answered before the guide could. "Until about three million years ago, all this was underwater." Anyone with a high-school grasp of geology could see that.

The tour guide continued to lead them around the park for the remainder of the afternoon. Asenath carried a small backpack, and just when Dylan thought he could go on no longer, she fished out two bottles of water and handed him one.

"Thanks." He unscrewed the plastic cap, took a swig, and recalled Holly's diatribe against water bottlers. The water was warm, but essential. When they stopped to buy his hat, he would purchase a refillable water bottle. Holly would never know, but he could imagine her approval.

Asenath handed him a tube of sunscreen. "You need to apply more."

"Thanks." He'd better add sunscreen to his shopping list. Part of learning to live in a different climate.

It was late when the tour ended. They were both famished. On the drive back to Cairo, Asenath pulled over at a roadside café. They drank limeade and ate falafels wrapped in flatbread. He checked his phone and finally had a signal. He resent his previous text to Holly: "Where are you? What are you doing?"

His phone chimed, and he looked at the screen.

"I'm working on my dissertation. Aren't you?"

What could he tell her, that he'd foolishly rushed to North Africa chasing after her and Atlantis? No. He replied with a smiley-face emoji and two hearts.

Dylan put his phone away. "So, this contract we sign . . . can someone just resign and go home?"

She wiped her mouth with a paper napkin. "No. The commitment is for six months. At that point, you can renew for six more. If you do, we give you a two-week paid vacation and round-trip airfare for you to visit your family. Bob Lansing should have made that clear before he let you sign up."

So, he was stuck here. He'd just have to do his bit and catch up with Holly six months from now. He checked his phone to see if she'd responded to his emojis. She hadn't.

Asenath dropped Dylan off at the guest house. "I'll pick you up on my way to the office in the morning. Eat breakfast here. Otherwise, you may not get any. Standard work week in Muslim countries is Sunday through Thursday, but our office may be a little crazy tomorrow because we have multiple volunteers arriving."

Dylan went to his room and took a hot shower to wash off the sunscreen and dust. He thought about the text exchange with Holly and consoled himself that if he was stuck here without her, at least he'd finagle a way to get to Morocco before he left Africa. He wondered how much the airfare from Cairo to Casablanca cost.

He removed his new wide-brimmed hat from the shopping bag, put it on, and looked at himself in the mirror. Indiana Jones? Not quite. But it'd keep the sun off his face.

Next, he took out his new Nalgene water bottle and rinsed it out. Too late, he wondered if the tap water here was safe to drink. Holy shit, had he just contaminated it? He read the label: "bpa free plastic." Okay, he could microwave it. He set it in the microwave and pushed the start button. One minute ought to kill anything in there.

He sighed. Welcome to North Africa.

Chapter 10
First Day at Work

When Asenath picked him up Sunday, she was dressed for business. Instead of a tee-shirt and jeans, she wore a crisp white blouse, dress slacks, and simple black flats. Her hijab was a conservative gray. She drove them to a low, modern, nondescript building, where they entered through a pair of glass doors. Inside were several work cubicles and a few offices with doors. Asenath deposited him in one of the offices with a young woman whom she said would go over some paperwork with him.

An hour later, Asenath returned. "You two finished?"

Dylan hoped so. His head was swimming with forms and fine print rules and protocols.

"I believe we are, Miss Kamel," the woman said.

"Good. Dylan, come with me."

Clearly, the tour guide was gone, replaced by the respected professional. He followed her into a small conference room where a ruddy-faced man in his early thirties was waiting. "Dr. Cote, this is Dylan Clarke. He will be joining you. Dylan, this is Dr. Benoit Cote, a hydrologist from Quebec."

"Call me Ben," Cote said as they shook hands.

"Gentlemen, please be seated." She turned off the room lights and turned on a projector.

Over the next twenty minutes, she talked about a central region in the Algerian desert called Tuat that contained a string of small oases.

"Groupement TouatGaz, a joint venture of Neptune Energy and Sonatrach, is currently developing eight gas fields near Adrar." She pointed out its location on the screen. "Of interest to us is a series of oases situated along the Wadi Messaoud that in the past provided water for camel caravans crossing the Sahara. These are found along the eastern edge of the Wadi and each supports a small village."

Dylan nodded. But why she was having him sit in on a presentation about Algeria?

"The area has almost zero annual rainfall. But Ben's studies have identified portions of the Touat where he believes the aquifer may be only two to six meters below the surface—ideal locations for community wells with hand pumps."

"Are these aquifers the remainder of ancient lakes?" Dylan said.

Ben nodded. "Oui. I'm surprised you know that."

"I'm a doctoral student in geophysics and climatology. I just attended a lecture on the Sahara at a symposium on desertification."

"Really? Excellent."

When Asenath turned on the lights, she looked relieved. "That's very good news, Dylan. Normally, we have new employees go through two weeks of orientation classes here before we send them into the field, just to give them some of the basics. But we're assigning you to our Algerian project and Ben's leaving for there this afternoon. How's your French?"

"I can probably translate written works—given a month and a good dictionary."

She frowned. "I don't suppose you speak Algerian, Arabic, or Berber."

"Nope."

"Well, then, it's a good thing you're going with Ben. French hasn't been an official language since Algeria's independence, but it's widely spoken and still taught in primary school. You two should be able to get along without Arabic."

So he was going to Algeria? Well, that was right next to Morocco. Maybe he'd be able to search for Atlantis on his days off.

She opened the conference room door. "We'll have a taxi take you to the guest house and wait while you pack your luggage. He'll bring you back and you'll leave from here after lunch." She offered Dylan her hand, and he shook it. "Now I regret not taking you to the pyramids yesterday. No one should leave Egypt without seeing them."

"That's all right. The whales were interesting."

"Really? I didn't get the impression you liked the tour."

"No, I enjoyed it. I was having trouble with my cell phone signal. A personal matter that had me distracted."

"I remember. I'll make a point to take you to the pyramids next time you're in Cairo."

"Next time?" He didn't know if there would be a next time. With Holly back in school, he planned to serve out his six-month contract and go home.

"Yes, we have quarterly meetings. You'll be back for that."

Oh. Well, at least he'd get to see the pyramids.

Chapter 11
A Babel of Tongues

Adrar was a good size city. Asenath had said about 65,000 people lived there. The Chinese had built a refinery about 40 kilometers north, but that didn't affect Ben and Dylan's work. What affected him most was that he didn't speak or read Arabic, and unless Ben was with him to translate the rapid, accented French to English, he couldn't understand a damn thing. It was like a neverending game of charades.

He and Ben had followed a truck mounted with a drilling rig from Cairo to Adrar, driving way too fast on nearly empty, dust-covered, two-lane highways across northern Egypt and Libya. Despite the crazy speeds, it took four brutal, twelve-hour days. The first two, they skirted the Mediterranean coastline and experienced occasional breezes. But somewhere around Al Bu'ayrat, Libya, the road turned inland, and they drove the rest of the way across vast expanses of dusty nothing. He knew the scope of the Sahara in his head, but seeing it in real life brought home just how massive it was.

In the weeks since they arrived, he'd mainly served as Ben's gofer, retrieving geologic maps from a case in the back of the Land Rover and watching Ben pick up and examine various rocks on the desert basin. Rocks, he understood, and eventually began to see what Ben was looking for—porous minerals that might hold water below the surface. The exchanges between the Berber well-drillers Algerian French and Ben's Canadian French, he did not.

Once a likely site was selected, Dylan put up a tent to shelter their equipment from the brutal sun. Meanwhile, Ben set up the compact, ultra-wideband Vivaldi antenna for the ground-penetrating radar. The first thing Dylan learned was that groundwater wasn't lying in underground lakes or flowing in underground rivers. In fact, it was simply water held in the porous subsurface rocks.

"These miniaturized, low-cost antennas compromise between depth and resolution," Ben said.

That required Dylan to relocate the antennas numerous times, while Ben compared findings from various locations. Again, Dylan slowly learned what he was looking for in the three-dimensional views of the subsurface. Well, at least there was a scientific basis to their work. They weren't walking around the desert holding a dousing stick.

If an area showed promise, the Berbers were called to bring the rig and drill test wells.

The people in outlying areas were strikingly poor. Unless they lived in an oasis, they could neither sow nor harvest. A productive well would change everything for them. That aspect of his work felt good.

Area oases grew plentiful date palms, and he indulged in the sweet fruit until he grew sick of it. But they seldom stayed in an oasis and rarely a city of any size. After all, those places already had water. Mostly they quartered in rural settlements just large enough to have a guest house. And from there, they commuted daily to an area where water was needed —consisting of a few rude houses amidst plentiful gravel and dust. Dylan would put up the tent, set up the equipment, watch Ben do what he did, try to memorize French verb declensions, and pack everything up at the end of the day.

Their workdays were long and days off seemingly non-existent. When he had time to go into a larger city, he found the squiggly Arabic signs unintelligible—almost as incomprehensible to him as the wavy lines on Ben's radar equipment. After a couple of weeks, he began learning that as well.

Ben was an affable co-worker who liked to spend their off hours quietly reading. Dylan had broached the subject of the Eye of the Sahara with him, hoping that would lead to a discussion of Atlantis. But Ben hadn't taken the bait. Dylan kept his laptop charged by plugging it into the Land Rover, but he seldom had access to the internet. So much for continuing his research while he was here.

The world here felt out of time—not in a good way—endless. Dylan had lost track of what week it was. Just to mark off the days, he bought a calendar that had twelve lunar months, but the year had only 355 days. He didn't care. He only had to be here six-months. No. Three. Asenath said they'd bring them back to Cairo for the quarterly meeting, whenever that was. He looked at the calendar but couldn't be sure. He just counted off weeks and outlined the twelfth with a red marker.

Chapter 12
Sandstorm

Dylan had just set the third ground-penetrating radar rod in the position to triangulate the field he was exploring when Ben's shadow appeared in his peripheral vision.

"Dylan?"

"Over here." Dylan connected the terminal ends of the cable to the rod and plugged the other ends into the portable signal generator.

Ben snapped off the power and disconnected the wires.

"What the hell, Ben? I haven't got the data yet."

"No time for that. The Algerian weather forecast has predicted a massive sandstorm with wind gusts of 100 kilometers per hour. We'll have to come back later." Ben pulled the antenna rods from the soil, and half-jogged to the Land Rover, dragging the still connected cables behind him. "Start taking down the tent. Don't be fussy about it. We need to go."

"You're in a real hurry."

Ben pointed toward the southeast and grabbed the signal generator. Dylan turned around. A mean yellow cloud spanned the width of the entire horizon and roiled high into the sky.

"Holy shit!"

"Oui," Ben said. "Get everything in the Land Rover."

The tent was more a pavilion, meant to shade them and their equipment. It was no protection against *that*. Dylan collapsed the foldable table they used to hold the instruments, and ran with it to the car, the table banging against his legs.

Ben dashed around the tent perimeter, pulling up guy ropes.

The wind picked up. Small sand drifts started to form around the wheels. Dylan jammed things into the vehicle willy-nilly. Last to go was the tent, which they simply rolled up into a wad of fabric.

Dylan pressed his shoulder against the spare tire attached to the rear door until he heard the door latch click. By the time he slid into the passenger seat, Ben had the engine running. The four-wheel drive engaged, and the tires spun for a second, spewing sand and gravel behind them before the vehicle surged forward. He was glad Ben was driving. His experience with Canadian blizzards would undoubtedly prove helpful.

They were still on the desert track—just a couple of ruts in the gravel— when the full fury of the storm hit them. Sand blasted the Rover from every direction, and visibility dropped to nothing. Ben turned on the windshield wipers, but they were no help. He shut them off and peered ahead. The sky above them took on a red tint, though it was hours before sunset.

Florida-born Dylan had never been in a blizzard, but he had ridden out hurricanes. The way the wind buffeted the vehicle and the fact that he couldn't see five feet in front of them gave him an unpleasant sense of déjà vu.

"Turn on the headlights," Dylan said.

"They're already on. It doesn't help."

Dylan depressed the four-way flasher switch. "No, but it may keep someone from running into us."

"Only if they're as lost as we are."

"Let's try this." Dylan brought up the vehicle's navigation system, entered the name of a small nearby village, and asked for directions. A static map of desert roads appeared. He waited. Nothing further happened. Evidently, the sandstorm was interfering with the GPS signals.

Dylan banged the screen with his palm. A red teardrop flashed on, indicating their location, followed almost immediately by a blue line on one of the roads.

Ben let the Rover crawl forward. "I can't tell if I'm on a road or the desert floor."

"Just keep to the blue line on the GPS," Dylan said. "I'll help you."

The Sahara was busy reshaping itself around them as winds from various directions created sand drifts in their path. Where these accumulated into miniature dunes, the Rover bounced over them, reminding Dylan of speed bumps.

Occasionally, the wind dropped, giving them brief glimpses of the surrounding landscape, and Ben would speed up. Then another gust would arise and envelop them in a swirling eddy of sand, forcing Ben to slow again. But whether the storm winds raged or waned, the sky kept its strange red hue.

Outside the window, dunes resembled cresting waves of dust. "Did you know that dust from this desert travels across the Atlantic Ocean to the Americas?" Dylan said, just to make conversation.

"I've heard that." Ben's grip on the steering wheel had the veins in the back of his hand bulging. He took one hand off the wheel and flexed his fingers, then switched hands and did the same for the other.

"Do you want me to drive for a while?"

"No. It's only twenty or thirty kilometers further."

"Something like that." Dylan glanced at the GPS screen. Ben was right, but the little red dot that was them barely moved. "You may as well relax. We can only go so fast, and we'll get there when we get there."

"You're right." Ben rolled his head, and Dylan heard his neck joints pop. Ben let out a deep sigh. "So, we've been making good progress with our mission, but I'm afraid I've been poor company. We haven't really talked about anything personal. What made you join the program?"

How should he answer that? Lie and say he was altruistic? It wasn't quite true, though Dylan was developing a taste for helping people, now that he'd met some of them. No. Ben was attempting to open up. He should tell the truth.

"Two reasons, actually. A woman, of course."

"Not Asenath!"

"What? No. She and I never met before I arrived in Cairo. Dr. Holly Johnson. She worked here last year, and I thought she was coming back, so I signed up to surprise her. But she didn't come. Maybe you remember her?"

Ben shook his head. "Afraid not. I help the foundation every couple of years, but it's sporadic. It's been two years since I've been here."

Dylan inhaled. The air in the car smelled dusty, but his brain ignored it and thought of Holly. What if she *had* come to Africa, and he was riding out the sandstorm with her instead of Ben?

"That must have been disappointing," Ben said. "You said two reasons. What was the other?"

He'd developed enough sense not to lead with Atlantis. "Geology. There is a geologic formation in the northwest Sahara called the Richat or Eye of the Sahara that I've wanted to investigate, possibly for my dissertation. I thought if I had a job in North Africa, I could just pop over there some weekend. But that hasn't worked out . . . yet."

"Sounds interesting. What's so special about it?"

He was tempted, so tempted. Just come out with it and they could spend the rest of the trip discussing something truly interesting. Hell, maybe Ben and he could fly there together for a long weekend. If the concentric rings that made up the Richat were truly water channels, a hydrologist might prove a very useful collaborator.

No. Stick to conventional science.

"Is there water there?" Ben said.

"No, not since the last wet period in the Sahara. Though at its western edge is a long, deep, chasm that may once have connected it to the Atlantic Ocean."

"Sounds like Plato's Atlantis," Ben said.

Dylan's heart fluttered. It really was that obvious. "You think so?"

"I said, 'Sounds like,' not *is*."

"Well, the thought occurred to me, too. Don't you want to go and find out?"

"You're joking."

"No. The Eye of Sahara is real. You can see it from space. And it does match Plato's description to a ridiculously detailed degree."

"Maybe, but that doesn't make a fable true."

"Nonetheless, it's a one-of-a-kind geological formation that I have to see for myself. And if you want to come along, nothing would please me more."

Ben shrugged. "Maybe. Let me see what Asenath says after all the wells are drilled."

Chapter 13
Tickets to Cairo

They eventually reached the small village where they holed up in a guest house. The sandstorm lasted three days. After it passed, Dylan and Ben returned to the site they'd been exploring and resumed the search for water. The dunes had shifted, building smaller dunes on top of older dunes. They almost didn't recognize the place, but for the GPS coordinates that were still in the navigation system's memory.

Once they got set up, Ben threw the switch and studied the waveforms on the portable scope.

"Anything?" Dylan said.

Ben shook his head.

They spent the day moving the antennas into different configurations without luck. "I would have sworn we'd find water here." Ben picked up the clipboard and drew a zero with a slash through it on the map. "Let's go. We'll try further east tomorrow. I'll help you pack the equipment. Neatly, this time."

The next morning, just after breakfast, Ben was checking messages on his computer. "Man, our first quarter is really flying by."

Dylan had often heard the Canadian say that, but from his perspective, the last three months had crawled.

Ben looked up from his computer screen. "Asenath Kamel just emailed us plane tickets. She's flying us back to Cairo for the quarterly meeting, instead of making us drive."

"Oh, yeah? That'll be a welcome change."

"I can't believe it's that time already."

Dylan could. He'd kept a calendar, x-ing out each day like a convict. And he still hadn't seen the Eye of the Sahara. "I don't especially want to go to Cairo. Why don't you represent both of us, and I'll take a few days to visit Morocco?"

Ben shook his head. "Can't do that. First, they're non-changeable e-tickets on the foundation's account. Second, the terms of our contract require everyone to attend the quarterlies."

Dylan frowned.

"You'll like it," Ben said. "Foundation throws a big to-do. You'll meet scientists working all over Africa."

"When do we go?"

"Three weeks."

Dylan checked his calendar. Not bad. His count was only off by a couple of days. With new data, he recalculated the end date of his contract and circled the day.

"I thought you'd be overjoyed about Cairo," Ben said. "Adrar doesn't exactly offer much excitement for a college student."

After almost three months of working together, did Ben think he was looking for Spring Break? Dylan wasn't that far from a doctorate himself. They'd be peers if he hadn't chased after Holly.

Or maybe Ben was saying that to sidetrack him from wanting to go to the Richat. Well, that wouldn't cut it. If he had to wait until the end of his contract to find Atlantis, he would.

* * *

Then, as the date for their flight neared, Dylan sensed a change in Ben. He'd catch Ben giving him sideway glances from time to time, or cutting their conversations a little short.

No point in letting it fester. Better to get it in the open now than at the quarterly meeting. "Something bothering you, Ben?"

"Since you brought it up . . . Yes. What you told me while we were driving through that terrible sandstorm . . . About the reason you are here . . ." Ben looked away. When he turned back, he locked eyes with Dylan. "I can't be here every year. I have a career to tend. But I and the other scientists who work for the foundation come back time after time because what we are doing here is important."

"And you think what I'm doing isn't?"

"You're looking for Atlantis."

"Look, I'm not searching for evidence of ancient aliens. There's a unique geological anomaly that matches Plato's descriptions. I just want to examine it before I leave Africa. And that doesn't mean I don't care about the people we're helping. I see what it means to bring wells to communities who need them. Just because a person has two motives doesn't mean his reasons are at cross-purposes. Asenath wants to show us the pyramids while we are here. Would you tell her that playing tourist for a day undermines her mission?"

Ben closed his eyes and sighed. "When we get to Cairo, you need to come clean to Asenath about your hidden agenda."

"I will. I don't think I have anything to be ashamed of." Though he was getting tired of saying that.

Chapter 14
Market Mishap

It started as an ordinary day. That morning, Dylan had squeezed, folded, and bent their last tube of toothpaste trying to get even a smidge on his toothbrush. Nothing. Finally, he jammed the bristles inside the opening with no better results.

Ben had taken the Land Rover to scout likely locations for their next well, so Dylan put on his hat and walked to the small collection of stalls that served as the village market. His Arabic was still mostly theoretical, and his French wasn't much better—he didn't get many chances to practice out in the desert. But he had a translator app on his phone, and his charades were pretty good.

Most of the stalls sold produce or grain or beans. But one wrinkled old man was selling soap and other sundries. Dylan scanned his table but saw nothing that looked like toothpaste. The man gave him a toothless smile that spoke volumes about dental hygiene.

"Parlez-vous francais?" Dylan ventured.

The old man smiled and shrugged.

He pulled out his phone and brought up the app, but apparently the remote rural village had no cell service. Attempting what had become his go-to solution, he pointed his phone toward the sky, waved it around, and turned in circles. Still no bars. And his limited Arabic vocabulary didn't include the word for teeth.

So, charades. He extended his index finger and rubbed his teeth horizontally. The man's eyes lit up. He reached under the table and brought out a toothbrush wrapped in plastic.

Dylan shook his head and pretended to squeeze toothpaste on his extended finger. The fellow didn't get it. After a few more attempts, he motioned for the man to give him the toothbrush. With that in hand, he pointed to the bristles and pantomimed applying toothpaste. That worked. After a losing haggle in which he had to buy a toothbrush he didn't need, to get the toothpaste which he did, he paid the man and turned to go.

The edge of a flat woven basket heaped with tomatoes struck him right in the gut.

The young woman carrying it shrieked. She was dressed in a haik, a traditional, veil-like garment that covered her from head to toe.

He grabbed the sides of the basket to steady it and keep her produce from spilling. In doing so, his hand tangled in the flowing fabric and, as she backed away, her veil was pulled off, revealing her face and hair.

She really screamed then.

Dylan let go, and the tomatoes spilled. An older woman next to her, whom Dylan assumed was her mother, frantically began fixing the daughter's garment, all the while shrilly jabbering at him in Arabic, or maybe Berber. The mother's face was covered except for her eyes, which were shooting daggers at him.

Dylan kneeled and began to pick up the tomatoes, wiping off the dirt and stacking them back on the basket. The young woman was still wailing, while the mother shouted at her, then at Dylan, then at the daughter again. This was bad.

It got worse.

Four bearded men suddenly surrounded him. Brothers, or maybe uncles? They pulled him upright by his elbows and pressed in close, squishing the tomatoes beneath their shoes. Dylan had no idea what would happen next, but it didn't look good. He tried to wiggle free of the men. Suddenly, he heard police whistles, and two of the local gendarmerie appeared. They separated the men from Dylan, and he took a deep breath. "Merci, Merci," he said.

Everyone talked at once, none of which he understood. "Parlez-vous anglais?" Dylan said over and over. No one paid him any attention. People continued to step on the tomatoes, which by this point were little more than a red smear in the dirt. After further discussion, the mother took her daughter and left. Then the gendarmerie bound his hands with a zip-tie.

"Hey! Wait a minute!"

They put him in a Jeep and drove him to a tiny stone building that must have been four-hundred years old. Inside, they sat him on a wooden chair, still zip-tied, and left.

In front of him was another gendarmerie whose desk was covered with papers held down by various small stones. On the corner of the desk, a small fan aimed toward the man's face caused the pages to flutter. He looked up and said something—in Berber, maybe.

Dylan shook his head. "Je ne comprends pas."

"Votre identification s'il vous plaît."

That was plain enough. The man wanted to see some ID, but that was in his pocket and he couldn't access it with his hands tied. He didn't speak that much French. How could he communicate the problem? He gestured toward his pants pocket with his head, repeatedly. That didn't do it. Finally, he said, "I'm an American. Americano. Comprenez vous?"

"Nom?"

"Dylan Clarke. This is all a mistake, I promise. I was only buying some toothpaste—"

The man held up his hand to cut him off and then lifted the handset of an old rotary phone that looked to be from the 1950s. He dialed a number, and when the other party answered, he rattled off instructions and hung up. Thereafter, he ignored Dylan and returned to his paperwork.

Time dragged. The plastic ties cut into Dylan's wrists. From time to time, he squirmed, trying to find the most comfortable position. Eventually, another gendarmerie walked in. The man behind the desk stood and saluted. The two had a lengthy conversation in Arabic.

The new arrival turned to Dylan. "I am Captain Saidi."

"You speak English!"

"Yes. You're American?"

"I am, and if you'll cut these things off my wrists, I'll be glad to show you my passport."

The captain picked up a pair of scissors from the desk, and in two snips, Dylan's hands were free.

Dylan opened the Velcro flap on his cargo pocket, removed his passport, and handed it to the captain, who thumbed through the pages, studying the entry and exit stamps while Dylan rubbed the red welts on his wrists.

"This place is hardly a tourist stop. What's your business here?"

Dylan fished out a card from his employer. "We're drilling community wells for remote villages. We have permission from the Algerian government. I was just trying to buy some toothpaste."

"Well, it doesn't get more remote that this place. These rural people are very conservative. You have humiliated a young woman and upset her family."

"It wasn't my fault. *She* ran into me. And I didn't remove her veil. It came off when she jerked away. I was only trying to help her hold on to her tomatoes."

"There's that, too. Loss and damage."

It might not be the best time to push back, but he'd had enough. "Now, wait a minute, please. That wasn't my fault either. I was on my hands and knees trying to pick them up for her when those men grabbed me. They and your gendarmeries are the ones who crushed them with their big feet. But if it will get me out of here, I'll be glad to pay for the tomatoes. Like I said, we're not here to hurt anyone. We just want to find them water."

The captain went to the door and said something to the men outside. When he returned, he handed Dylan the toothbrush and toothpaste he'd dropped in the skirmish.

"My family comes from a small village like the ones you're helping," he said. "I know what this work means to them." He gave him back his passport, but kept the business card. "You're free to go."

Dylan hoped the man wasn't going to call Cairo. He'd rather that Asenath never heard about this incident. Of course, if Ben found out, he'd likely feel obligated to tell her.

Ben was at the hotel when he got back. "I wondered where you'd gone."

"To the market—we ran out of toothpaste."

Chapter 15
The Quarterly Meeting

It was after midnight when they parked the Rover at Adrar's small airport to board a 2 a.m. flight to Algiers. Not Dylan's favorite time to fly, but the connecting flight from Algiers to Cairo left at 8:30 in the morning. Even with the early start, the Algiers to Cairo flight took almost four hours. Although he caught a few catnaps by the time they landed, he felt exhausted.

Asenath waved from the arrival gate, her cheery face wrapped in an azure hijab. She wore a tight-fitting suit jacket over a white silk blouse and dark dress slacks.

The three exchanged greetings, and she shook their hands. "We have to wait for the team from Chad. Their flight should land soon. We can get lemonade while we wait."

He and Ben followed her to an airport kiosk that had small, round tables. Asenath pointed them toward an empty table and went to the counter to buy their drinks. She returned, carrying three tall waxed paper cups dripping condensation, and took her seat. "The foundation is pleased with what you've accomplished. New wells in twelve communities— impressive for your first three months. Now, for your reward, I know there wasn't time to see the pyramids when you were here before, so I've booked a tour after the conference."

The quarterly meeting was more fun than Dylan expected, and bustling Cairo was a welcome change from Adrar. The scientists working on projects in neighboring countries were, for the most part, empathetic academics who had taken a sabbatical to do a little field work. They came from a wide range of specialties, and conversations tended toward an intellectual level he hadn't experienced since the symposium at UF. Over the course of the meetings, he began to think of himself as an academic on a sabbatical, too. And that's the way he'd list it on his *Curriculum Vitae*.

One thing the quarterly meeting made clear was that extreme weather events caused by climate change affected poor people disproportionately. Floods contaminated water supplies, and droughts reduced ponds and scoop holes, where the poor got their water to muddy patches. Middle-class and rich people could weather a disaster by stocking up on bottled water. The poor didn't have that option. They also lacked information about where to find relief, and too often, they migrated thousands of miles, only to be stopped at the border of a country that didn't want them. This created slum border camps lacking any sanitation services.

By the final meeting, he had an even better understanding of how the wells his and Ben's team had drilled made a difference. And he began to feel, as Ben did, that there was nobility and worth to what they were doing. Who knew? Someday, when his and Holly's careers were as established as Ben's, they might come back regularly to help. But next time as a couple.

Another thing he picked up on was the need to train local people how to maintain the pump once it was up and working. Illiteracy was high, so you couldn't just leave a product manual and drive away. It now became evident why they'd completed more wells than the other teams. They'd just been punching holes in the earth, driving pipes down, attaching a hand pump, and leaving. When they returned to Algeria, he'd have to revisit each site and set up a maintenance-training program that the people could continue on their own.

He caught Ben's arm as they were leaving an afternoon session. "Can we talk?"

"Oh, hi, Dylan. Maybe later. I'm on my way to meet some colleagues for a drink."

"I thought you couldn't buy alcohol in Muslim countries."

"It's not illegal in Egypt. Most hotels and restaurants sell it." Ben turned to go.

"Hold on. This won't take long. I just wanted to say I talked to Asenath about my interest in Atlantis, and she's fine with it."

Ben shrugged.

"Also, I'm sorry for anything I said that created distance between us. We're a team, and the work we're doing is important. I want you to know that, for the time I have left, I'm going to give one hundred percent."

"Dylan, I never thought you were slacking. I just thought you weren't being forthright with Asenath."

"Well, I am now."

"Then all is well." Ben looked at his watch and then at the door. "Listen, if you want to come along, I'm sure another academic won't matter."

"Thanks, but I have plans. I just wanted to clear the air before tomorrow."

"Tomorrow?"

"You, I, and Asenath are spending the day touring pyramids, and I didn't want you wondering if you should or shouldn't say something to her."

"That's very considerate," Ben turned to go. "Sorry, I'm late. Are you sure you won't join us?"

Dylan waved. "See you in the morning."

Chapter 16
Trip to the Pyramids

Shaved and dressed, Dylan met Ben for breakfast while they waited for Asenath to pick them up. Today, the guesthouse offered a selection of Egyptian salads, baladi bread, falafel, and spiced cooked fava beans. It was both exotic and delicious.

He'd been unsure if the tour was indoors or out, so before he left his room, he'd slathered sunscreen over every inch of exposed skin. He'd also brought his hat and water bottle. Asenath would see that he had learned something about the desert since the last time he was here.

She arrived looking relaxed now that the quarterly meeting was over. The men stood, and Dylan offered her a chair. "Will you join us for a coffee?"

She looked at her watch and shook her head. "Tourists start crowding in around ten o'clock. We want to be there when the gates open at eight." As they walked to her car, she said, "Dylan, I notice you're tanner."

"Nah, my freckles have just melted and run together. Curse of us redheads."

Ben took the passenger seat, so Dylan got in the back.

"We're not going far, only about 24 kilometers," Asenath said. "The Giza plateau is near the ancient city of Memphis, which was one of the oldest and most important cities in Khem—that's the original name for Egypt. Its location at the entrance to the Nile River Valley made it the ideal site for the capital and an important religious center. After we tour the Giza pyramids, we can drive out to Saqqara, where the oldest known pyramid was built."

Dylan slid to the center of the seat so he could look out the windshield between Asenath and Ben's shoulders. He'd seen the Great Pyramid from the highway on his previous trip, for it and its two companions stood out and were lit with bright floodlights at night. He'd read they could even be seen from the space station.

This time, after ten minutes of driving, the Sphinx came into view. It was . . . stunning. He'd seen pictures. Who hadn't? But up close and in person was different. The face he estimated to be about six stories tall and the body easily two or three football fields long. Then Asenath turned onto the road to the tourist parking area and he lost sight of it.

"That's really something," Ben said.

"Its head must be as big as those on our Mount Rushmore," Dylan said.

Asenath nodded. "And like the presidents on your monument, the Sphinx is carved out of a single rock." She parked. "Cars aren't allowed beyond this point. There's a shuttle that will take us the rest of the way."

They got out. She locked the car and showed the tour guide their reservation. He put a check by her name on his clipboard. "Please board the bus. We'll be proceeding shortly."

Good. Their guide spoke English.

When the bus was fully loaded, the guide boarded last and began his spiel. He spoke with a crisp British accent. "Here stand the oldest of the Seven Wonders of the ancient world, and the only wonder still in existence." The guide pointed to the largest of the three pyramids. "It is called the Great Pyramid, and for over 4500 years it was the tallest building on earth. Originally, it was 481 feet high, with smooth sides made of polished limestone and black onyx. Its covering stones were removed in 1356 AD and used to construct mosques. But you can imagine how brightly it must have gleamed. The loss of its outer casing reduced its height to 450 feet."

The bus let them off, and the group walked to the base of the Great Pyramid. Other tourists arrived in small horse carts and some on camels.

"The sides rise at an angle of 51 degrees, 52 minutes and are 755 feet long. The base of the Great Pyramid covers thirteen acres."

Dylan craned his neck but could not see the apex. Standing next to the base, he grasped for the first time the enormity of the sandstone blocks that had once been hidden beneath the sheath of limestone. They ranged from chest-high to well over his head. It was humbling.

And how had they done it? He kept insisting that his interest in Atlantis had nothing to do with ancient astronauts, and technologically sophisticated lost civilizations. He'd seen speculation on how the pyramids could have been built with hand tools, ramps, and a lot of dedication. But looking at them . . . he could see the sense behind some of the History Channel specials.

"The Great Pyramid contains two point three million blocks of stone," the guide said. "The weight of each ranges from two-and-a-half tons to fifteen tons. The joints between them, vertical and horizontal, are not more than two millimeters wide."

The guide spoke with such pride one would think he'd done the work himself.

"This pyramid was built by the pharaoh Khufu." He chuckled. "Well, not by Khufu himself, but during his reign. Estimates run from thirty- to one hundred-thousand workers over a span of twenty years."

"Don't you mean slaves?" said one of the tourists.

"Actually, that's a misconception. According to studies by National Geographic, most or all of the builders were paid Egyptian masons, craftsmen, and quarry men."

"How could ancient Egyptians, who had only soft copper tools, have quarried and shaped solid rock?" said a man in their group. "And how could they lift the block to such heights?"

"They didn't," said another. "According to Joseph Davidovits, a professor at the Geopolymer Institute in France, they were cast in place using a slurry of dissolved limestone, lime, sodium bicarbonate, and tecto-alumino-silicate-forming materials carried up in buckets. These bonded by geochemical reaction into hardened re-agglomerated limestone indistinguishable from natural stone."

Dylan and Ben, who knew geology well, leaned in and studied the stones. They looked like classic limestone. If they were manmade, the technique was beyond anything that could be manufactured today.

The tour guide wiped sweat from his brow. "That's only a hypothesis—and not a very popular one at that." He swung his arm in a line to the sun. "Another unique fact about all three pyramids on this plain and, for that matter, all pyramids in Egypt, is that their corner points accurately align with the four cardinal directions."

A young Egyptian man about Dylan's age approached and signaled the guide.

"Ah, it's our turn to go inside," the guide said. "Please show this man your entry ticket and follow him."

"Asenath turned to Dylan and Ben. "Hang on, you haven't seen anything yet."

Chapter 17
Inside a Pyramid

Asenath leaned toward them and whispered, "I should have asked before I bought the tickets, but are either of you claustrophobic?"

Ben shook his head.

"I'll be fine," Dylan said. Actually, he wasn't crazy about tight spaces, but this was the Great Pyramid, for God's sake!

Asenath checked her hijab to make sure it was tightly in place. "First, there's a challenging bit of a climb."

They ascended the outside of the pyramid by climbing stone steps cut between the huge limestone building blocks.

"It's illegal to climb on pyramids except at this entrance," said their Egyptian guide. "If you get caught climbing elsewhere, the police will arrest you."

Dylan's mind snapped back to his arrest in the market. No thanks.

The entrance was a cleft in the rocks about eight feet wide and eleven feet tall. A man wearing a navy-blue uniform with shoulder epaulets sat on a wooden stool, watching the queue of tourists.

"This is the Robbers' Entrance," their guide said. "Excavated at the command of a ninth century Caliph searching for riches. To his disappointment, the pyramid contained no treasure."

Once inside, they walked sixty or seventy feet, then reached a small tunnel where they had to get down on all fours. Now he understood why Asenath had told them to wear jeans.

Inside the tunnel, Dylan felt a quick wave of panic, as if, after several millennia, the whole two-million-ton structure might finally collapse at this moment. Ahead of him, Asenath crawled behind their guide, seemingly unafraid. Behind him, Ben and the other members of their tour blocked his retreat. Nothing to do but take a deep breath and scuttle forward. When they reached the tunnel end and could stand up again, he felt pleased with how he'd handled himself.

There was a horizontal passage to their left. "That leads to the Queen's Chamber, but it is presently closed," the guide said. No indication of why.

Next, they turned up a steep slope. Wood planks had been laid across it, and wooden handrails put up to make something like a stairway. "This is the Grand Gallery. It is ten meters high and fifty meters long."

Yeah, but only two meters wide. He was still feeling a bit claustrophobic.

"The ceiling of the Grand Gallery is a corbelled arch with an angle of 26 degrees." The guide swept the beam of a high-intensity flashlight along the ceiling. "To construct a corbelled arch, the ancient builders stacked each successive layer of stones slightly overhanging the ones below it until they met at the peak. Each upper stone holds the one below it in place."

In other words, nothing was holding the ceiling together except gravity! Great.

"The Gallery walls are granite slabs brought from Aswan and weigh up to fifty tons each."

The passage walls were without decoration—no murals, no carving, no hieroglyphics. As they went higher, smaller horizontal passages intersected, but wire-mesh gates blocked access to them. The air smelled hot and stale. It reminded him of driving past a road crew laying asphalt.

At the upper end of the Gallery passage, Dylan stepped into a hot, dark stone room. It wasn't small or claustrophobic—it was actually pretty majestic. But it was empty.

"This is the King's Chamber," their guide said.

Dylan wondered who decided that. The walls were plain. Wouldn't Khufu's tomb contain hieroglyphs of his life and deeds?

"The ancient Egyptians were sophisticated architects and skilled astronomers. Not only do all the Giza pyramids point in the cardinal directions, the pyramids also align with the constellations."

There wasn't much to see except an empty no-frills sarcophagus that reminded him of a large granite bathtub. Dylan hung back near the wall.

"This is the most important room in the Great Pyramid," the guide said. "I will give you some time to enjoy it."

Asenath came over to Dylan and whispered, "Stand in the middle of the room where the sarcophagus is. It's the exact center of the pyramid."

He walked over and peered into the sarcophagus. Asenath came with him.

She nudged his back with her elbow. "Put your hands on it."

"Is that allowed?"

"Yes."

Dylan rested his palms on the cool stone rim and . . . he slipped into what he could only describe as a meditative trance. It was as if his body vibrated in tune with a subtle field of energy.

After a few moments, his knees weakened, and he faltered. Asenath took him by the arm and led him away.

What the hell had just happened to him?

"I need to go outside. The air in here is stifling," he said, knowing full-well that was just an excuse. As a scientist, he didn't believe in ghosts or psychic phenomena, but boy, if he did—

"Just wait here against the wall for the others. We'll go soon." She left him and returned to the sarcophagus. She laid her own hands on it. A faraway look came in her eyes and a small smile played at the corner of her lips.

Dylan took a deep breath to calm his mind. Whatever he'd felt was less intense over here. His scientific curiosity began to kick in. He slowly worked his way around the room to see if proximity mattered, but before he got very far, the guide said their time was up.

They left the pyramid by the same route they had entered. This time, crawling through the tunnel seemed slightly less claustrophobic. Outside, the desert was hot and dusty, but above him was open sky. A shiver of excitement coursed through him. He'd been inside the Great Pyramid! A once-in-a-lifetime experience, one he'd talk about for years. Not one he planned to repeat. But it was enough to make him believe some of the crazier stuff about Atlantis.

They slogged through thick sand to a smaller pyramid. "This was built by Pharaoh Menkaure, Khufu's grandson." It was midmorning now, and tourists swarmed like ants around a discarded sweet. Their group decided to forego the queue waiting to enter Menkaure's pyramid, so the guide led them to the other large pyramid.

"This pyramid is the second oldest of the three major pyramids at this site," the guide said. "From a distance, it appears to be the same height as the Great Pyramid, but it is actually shorter. Unfortunately, the interior is closed today so we cannot go inside to see its massive 400-ton granite ceiling."

That suited Dylan. "Can we see the Sphinx?"

"We're going there next," the guide said. "It's on the other side of this pyramid. In fact, the head of the Sphinx is believed to be the face of Khufu's son, Khafre."

Tourists were even thicker around the Sphinx, taking selfies standing between its paws. Asenath pointed out it'd been five hours since breakfast and suggested they have lunch at a place across the road called the Pyramids Restaurant. She recommended the "mixed grill plate," which proved delicious and satisfying. After they had eaten, they walked back to the entrance gate and caught the shuttle back to the car park.

Twenty minutes later, they reached Saqqara. "These are some of Egypt's first pyramids," she said as she parked the car. "This is where it all began."

Dylan saw eleven step pyramids whose shape reminded him of pyramids outside Mexico City. Instead of smooth sides, the pyramids consisted of five tiers diminishing in size up to the apex, which he estimated was about 200 feet high. Looking at them, it was hard to see them as a beginning. They already seemed part of a fully formed civilization. The civilization that Egyptian geoarchaeologist Fekri Hassan suggested had migrated east from the mega-lakes as the Sahara turned into desert. The civilization whose name he dared not speak, at least in scientific company.

He thought of Alfred Wegener, the meteorologist who had proposed back in 1912 that the continents had once been joined. His theory was often dismissed despite the obvious evidence. It wasn't hard to imagine the same thing happening now, over Atlantis.

While they were there, they visited the Imhotep museum. A friendly docent, who spoke decent English, informed them that Imhotep had been the architect of the first pyramid. "Imhotep was chancellor to Pharaoh Djoser, for whom the pyramid was built. Imhotep served as high priest to the sun god Ra and was one of the few non-royals to be deified after death."

The museum had six halls displaying archaeological finds from various excavations on the Saqqara plateau—ancient tools, Egyptian art, and statues. As they explored them, Ben kept checking his phone. Finally, he said, "Asenath, do you mind taking me back to the guesthouse? I have a web conference with my university that begins in an hour."

"Certainly," she said. "Dylan and I are going to dinner. Do you want us to bring you some takeout?"

"Thank you, that'd be nice. Anything you choose will be fine."

During the drive back, Dylan wondered if there were remains of pyramids out at the Richat.

Chapter 18
Common Ground?

After Asenath dropped Ben at the guesthouse, she took Dylan to a small, local eatery, not frequented by tourists and more likely to serve genuine, Egyptian cuisine. They ordered, and while waiting for their meal, she said, "I don't usually bring this up with most scientists I take to the pyramids. But . . . you felt it. Didn't you?"

"What?"

"When we were in the Great Pyramid . . . in the King's chamber . . . You could feel something. I did too. I often have when I've gone there."

Dylan toyed with his silverware and took a sip of water. He had experienced something, but . . . pyramid power was a little far out, even for him.

"You're skeptical, I know," she said. "From a scientist, I expect that. It's the reason I seldom broach the topic. But the other day you mentioned Atlantis, so I'm going to take a leap and assume you're open to unconventional ideas."

Did Asenath know something about Atlantis? "Have you read Hübner's papers?"

"Who?"

"Michael Hübner. He wrote about the . . . never mind. You were saying?"

She glanced around and lowered her voice. "I experience a subtle, but profound, energy every time I take guests inside the King's Chamber, and today, I sensed it happen to you."

"Don't tell me you believe it's haunted by Khufu's ghost."

"Don't be silly. No one was ever entombed there. I'm talking about something completely different. Think of a prism. It's actually a transparent pyramid, isn't it?"

He nodded.

"Well, just the way a prism bends light to into separate wavelengths we call colors, the geometric shape of a pyramid refracts all frequencies of energy, not just the visible spectrum."

"You're talking about Pyramid Power. That's pretty much been debunked."

"Look, I'm not saying it sharpens razor blades or whatever charlatans in the past claimed, but that chamber is definitely the focal point of the pyramid. And it seems the focal point for a sort of higher frequency energy, as well."

"You mean cosmic rays."

"I don't know. But whatever that frequency of energy is called, the pyramid concentrates it in a way that's palpable to you, me, and thousands who came before us."

Dylan *was* skeptical. It must have shown on his face.

"Serious scientists believe in cosmic rays, too." She smiled. "Five years ago an international collaboration between a Paris institute and the

Egyptian Ministry of Antiquities measured high-energy particles produced by cosmic rays from space passing through the Great Pyramid. Their study identified a previously unknown chamber about a hundred feet above the Grand Gallery. The results were published in *Scientific American* and *National Geographic*."

Dylan nodded. He remembered when the articles came out. Back then, Egypt wasn't really his concern, and he'd pushed it out of mind.

"Several universities from Japan re-scanned the Great Pyramid in 2020 using a newly developed muon detector, but their results haven't been published yet."

"Well, now that I've been inside, I'd be interested in reading what they found."

"I'll text you when it comes out," she said.

"Please do."

"In line with my analogy of a prism, I suspect the other vaults, like the Queen's Chamber and this new one the Japanese discovered, render energy differently based on their position within the structure. What you experienced didn't come from resting your hands on the sarcophagus. It happened because you were closer to the pyramid's exact center. I've often thought if you could climb inside the sarcophagus and lie down, you'd get the full effect."

"That'd be a little creepy, lying in some dead guy's coffin."

Asenath laughed. "Oh, the guards would never allow it. But here's what's interesting about these three pyramids. None of the three pharaohs who built them were ever interred in them. In fact, there's no evidence these three pyramids were ever used as tombs by anyone."

"I thought they were."

"No. Think about the corridors inside the Great Pyramid, the ones we crawled through. Men never could have carried a pharaoh's sarcophagus thorough them. The pharaoh would have had to be put in first, and then the pyramid built around him. That's not how any of them were built."

Dylan scratched his head. "Then why build a big stone receptacle for a sarcophagus in the King's Chamber?"

"My guess is it was there for some sort of ritual immersion in cosmic rays by priests and initiates of the Egyptian Mystery Schools."

"But . . . the older pyramids you showed us in Saqqara were actual tombs. Doesn't that wreck your theory?"

"The ancient Egyptian religious cults were invested in their beliefs about one's journey in the afterlife. Perhaps once the Egyptian priests realized that pyramids' concentrated energy, they decided to make tombs in that shape. They probably figured it would give the soul of the deceased a little boost on its way to the next plane."

"That's a very . . . interesting theory."

"Is that a polite way of saying you think I'm crazy?"

"No, but you're wise not to share these ideas with every scientist the foundation brings to Cairo. Believe me, I know."

She laughed. "Only ones who come looking for Atlantis."

He hid his blush by taking a drink of water.

Still, her theory sparked his curiosity. Nothing he'd read suggested Atlantis had pyramids, but nothing said they hadn't. And the Richat was a big place. Had anyone ever looked for, say, a bedrock foundation oriented to the cardinal points?

Chapter 19
Dylan's Idea

The next day, Dylan and Ben flew back to Algeria. Ben left Dylan to set up the pump maintenance training for communities where they'd already drilled wells, while he picked up where they'd left off in their search for new sites. This division of labor made no sense to Dylan. Although he'd learned a smattering of Arabic and enough French to cause trouble in the market, he by no means had mastered either sufficiently to teach, particularly something as filled with technical terms as pump maintenance. Why not Ben, a Quebec-Canadian who spoke French naturally?

The pump manufacturer's product manual came as a PDF with sections in English, Spanish, and French. Dylan printed out the French section and thought he'd have the villagers read along as he showed them what to do. It didn't work. Men in the first community he tried had decided that wells were women's responsibility. Unfortunately, the women couldn't read French even though some spoke it.

Dylan emailed the manufacturer and asked if they had a version in Arabic. They didn't. He phoned Asenath to ask if she could translate the manual into Arabic. He wouldn't be able to read it, but the women could.

"That may not work, either," she said. "In many remote villages, girls' reading lessons are aimed at memorizing one twelfth of the Quran by heart, so an Arabic manual may be beyond their reading level. I'm glad you're trying new ideas, though. Keep up the good work. I have confidence you'll find a way."

She did? Why? It didn't seem he'd done much so far but move equipment around and yearn for his six months to be up.

One night in Adar, he ate dinner in a new restaurant. He couldn't read the menu, but it had photos of the food choices and he ordered by pointing.

Eureka!

While he ate, he visualized a graphic instruction manual. When he returned to his room, he started a blank document on his laptop. From the manufacturer's PDF manual, he copied images and pasted them into it. He searched the internet for drawings of a screwdriver, a wrench, and an Allen wrench. He used frowning and smiley memes for "do" and "don't." Where the manufacturer didn't have precisely the picture he needed, he took photos of a disassembled pump with his phone and downloaded them to his computer. He saved the finished document as a PDF, and the next day took it to the one place in town that had a color printer.

Quite pleased with the result, he tested the women's ability to perform routine maintenance using only his picture book. He kept notes where he needed additional photos or where part of an image needed to be enlarged to show more detail. His idea was working until the pages got wet and the ink ran.

How stupid of him. Pumps were meant to move water.

Undaunted, he added the necessary changes to the file and then emailed it to Asenath, asking her to have the pages printed, laminated, and put in three-ring binders.

"Wonderful idea," she wrote back.

A week later, he received a box from Cairo containing twenty-five manuals. With these, he was able to move quickly through the remaining communities, and within a month, had caught up to Ben with a dozen manuals left.

"Symbolic instructions. Nice," Ben said when Dylan showed him what he'd created. "Sort of modern hieroglyphics of pump maintenance."

"Maybe the ancient Egyptians knew better than we," Dylan said. "In conditions of non-literacy, the best way to transmit important information might be pictures and symbols."

"Well, I'm glad to have you back with me," Ben said. "With two of us searching for water and your new picture books for training, we'll be able to resume our previous pace."

Dylan laughed. "With this, the other teams will be able to keep up with us." Still, he thought, it was all for the greater good.

Chapter 20
Sleepless Call to Action

Electricity for the small village hotel he and Ben were staying in was subject to brown-outs and sometimes blacked out completely. Such was the case tonight. Without a working air conditioner, his room was stifling. He opened the window, but according to his phone, the outdoor temperature was still 81 degrees.

Since he and Ben had separate rooms, he stripped naked and lay on the bare bottom sheet. He tried to visualize some place cool, and his mind naturally turned to the Ichetucknee River, its water a constant 72 degrees year-around. And from there, it naturally turned to Holly. They'd floated downstream on inner tubes. Holly wore her favorite string bikini—his favorite as well.

It was the summer before she left for England. Temperatures in Gainesville had been hovering in the high nineties. The difference was that in Florida rained every afternoon. Although, truth be told, the rains seldom dropped the temperature more than fifteen degrees and raised the humidity equally. Holly joked that soon she'd be in much cooler England.

"But more rain," he teased back.

She dipped her hand in the turquoise water and splashed him. He didn't mind. It was invigorating.

He turned over on his tube and dipped his face in the water. His sunglasses slid off and were carried forward by the two-mile-per-hour current. Dylan rolled off the inner tube and gave chase. The river was only five feet deep in most places and crystal clear. He quickly spotted them, grasped, and missed. His fingers clasp them on the second try. When he surfaced, he swam to Holly, who had hold of his tube. "Thanks. I don't know what I'll do after you're gone."

"I expect you'll lose both your sunglasses and the inner tube."

He shifted the memory in a different direction, lest it become maudlin. They saw a pair of wood ducks balanced on a log near the bank. The male, rosy-breasted, had a green crested head and colorful blue plumage on his back; his mate had a patch of similar blue feathers on her back, but the rest of her was a drab tan. The ducks watched without alarm as Dylan and Holly drifted past.

Holly flipped onto her stomach, adjusting her bikini bottom after doing so. Something about that simple action aroused him. He grabbed the rope on her tube and pulled it close. They kissed and laughed and drifted onward.

He slipped into slumber with a smile on his face, and didn't wake until the 4:30 a.m. call to prayer. Allahu Akbar, indeed.

He'd grown used to the daily blaring announcement and usually didn't hear it. Maybe tonight was due to the window being open or the sound of the air conditioner starting as the electricity came back on. He tossed and turned, unable to conjure up another dream. Even Holly couldn't help him now.

After another restless hour, he got up, showered, and shaved. Six o'clock was too early to wake Ben. No reason for them both to lose sleep. He got out his calendar and drew an X through another square. Only three weeks remained. Any day, Ben would start talking about the upcoming quarterly meeting, and Asenath would send plane tickets. Since he had no intention of extending his contract, he hoped she wouldn't require him to attend. He was learning a lot, but he had other things to do. An unnecessary trip back to Cairo would only take him farther from the Eye of the Sahara.

Dylan picked up his phone. It was two hours later in Cairo. Would Asenath be at the office yet? He wasn't so ill-mannered as to resign by text. Better to do it face to face. But he could send a text to request a video conference. Let her answer it when she got in.

Suddenly, he was more edgy than if he'd drunk three cups of coffee. After reading about it for more than a year, he might actually get there. *Atlantis, here I come.*

His phone dinged. She'd texted back: "I have time now. Do you want to FaceTime?"

"Can't," he texted. "My phone's an android. Can you set up a Zoom meeting?"

"Yes. Give me a sec."

Dylan looked around the room. Packing would be a breeze. He hadn't bought much beyond necessary sundries. He wasn't into souvenirs, not that there was anything in the marketplaces that interested him. The whole time he'd been here, they'd lived like nomads, moving from one settlement to the next. It kept their baggage light.

His phone chimed, and he glanced at the text. She'd sent a link. He clicked it and then clicked Join Meeting. Her brown eyes and warm smile filled the screen. She leaned back and he could see her dark hair falling over her shoulders. No hijab? Must be calling from home.

"Hello, Dylan. Nice to see you. Can you hear me?"

"Loud and clear. I hope it's not too early."

"It's not. How is Algeria?"

"Hot. How's Cairo?"

"Wet. It's raining here."

"Seriously? Does that happen often?"

"Almost never. Only a few times a year. The neighborhood kids are all outside playing in it."

Did she have children? He realized he wasn't even sure if she was married. He didn't think so, but he'd never asked. The most personal thing he knew about her was that she believed pyramids bent cosmic rays. To be fair, she'd been right. He'd Googled the thing about the muon detectors and the previously unknown chamber, and it was all legit.

"So, what's up?" she said. "You didn't call to talk about the weather."

"My contract ends this month, and I'm sorry, but I'm not going to renew it."

"I figured."

"Don't take it personally, please. You've been great, and thank you for going beyond the job—showing me the whale fossils, and Cairo, and the pyramids."

She smiled. "I enjoyed showing them to you. I'll be sorry to see you go."

"That's the thing. While it'd be great to see you, I'd like to skip the quarterly meeting and return to the states via Morocco."

She frowned.

He pressed on. "The cost to the foundation for plane fare to the US from Morocco shouldn't be much different than flying me to Cairo, then home from there. It might even be less."

"Oh, we'll pay to send you home—that's in your contract. And I suppose Ben Cote could present the quarterly report for both of you. But why Morocco?"

"There's a geologic formation, the Richat, or the Eye of the Sahara, that I've wanted to visit since I got to North Africa."

"You told me about it at the last quarterly meeting. But Dylan, it's in Mauritania, not Morocco."

"Really? He'd never noticed the national borders when he'd looked at Google maps.

"Yeah, a couple hundred miles south of Morocco. But it's not a tourist destination."

"That's okay. Would the foundation send me home via Mauritania instead of Cairo?"

She was silent, but the microphone picked up the tapping of her fingernails as she drummed her fingers on the table in front of her laptop.

Well, if she said no, he had savings. Lord knows there hadn't been anything to spend his stipend on in Adrar. It'd be a big time waster, though. An extra round trip just so they could fly him home from Cairo.

Asenath shrugged. "I don't believe in making things difficult for our volunteers. Unhappy alumni make it tough to recruit more scientists. I'll look into flights for you. We'll probably have to route your flight home through Lisbon."

The tension he'd been holding melted. "That's fine. Great, in fact."

"Promise me you'll say kind words about our program, though."

"Of course I will. And mean every word of it. Asenath, you're the best, and the times we've been together were a genuine pleasure."

She blushed and turned away from the camera. When she looked back, her eyes tracked back and forth across the screen, and he heard typing. They were still connected, but he recognized that she had brought up her browser and was searching for something.

"Oh, Dylan! Mauritania is unsafe to travel. Westerners, especially, are frequent targets of robbery and kidnapping."

"Well, I'm only going to be there long enough to examine the Richat and take some photographs."

"Is it worth risking your life?"

"Why would anybody want to kidnap me? I'm a nobody, an underpaid grad student. Besides, I can't change the location of the Richat. I have to go where it is."

"Sounds foolish. Let me ask if the foundation can vet a reliable local to drive you and provide security."

"My personal driver? I'm hardly a President or CEO."

"I insist. Volunteers arriving home in body bags really puts a dent in recruiting."

He laughed. She didn't.

"You also need a visa to enter the country. Let me give you some advice. When you apply, don't mention you're with an NGO. A lot of African countries are suspicious of NGOs and may think you're a missionary or a spy. Just tell them you're a geology student on holiday and want to see this Richat. Same thing when you go through immigration. You're simply a tourist there for a short visit."

"That's absolutely true." Probably best not to tell them he was searching for Atlantis, either.

"Well, I'm sorry to lose you. I'll set things in motion and get back to you as soon as possible."

"Asenath, again, you're the best."

"Be safe, my friend." She signed off.

He clicked the End Meeting button and closed the app. He started to text Holly to tell her he'd be home by the end of the month, then remembered he'd never told her he'd followed her to Africa.

Better to let that wait until he returned home with photographic proof of the site of Atlantis.

Chapter 21
Mauritania

Dylan's driver was waiting for him as he exited Mauritania immigration. The man handed him a laminated photo ID issued by the security firm —Uthman Salik. Dylan fumbled in his computer bag and pulled out a fax and compared Uthman's picture to the grainy, muddled, black-and-white image on the fax. Close enough. He thought it was all a bit of overkill anyway, but when he'd said that to Asenath, she blanched and said, "Don't say 'kill.' The idea frightens me."

Uthman nodded when Dylan handed him back his ID. "Good. Caution is good."

Dylan followed him outside to a Land Rover. Uthman took Dylan's bag, put it in the back, closed the rear hatch, and locked it with a padlock.

Really? What would a thief get? Yesterday's underwear and a few pairs of clean slacks.

Dylan got in the front seat and held his computer bag on his lap. Uthman got in the driver's side and reached for the computer. "That needs to be stored in back. Your smartphone as well."

He hesitated. "Can I ask why?" Maybe Asenath's concerns were justified. What if he really was being kidnapped? No phone, no computer, no way to tell anybody what became of him.

"Many checkpoints along the roadway," the driver said. "Some guards will confiscate anything they can sell on the black market." He made air quotes around confiscate. "Where is your passport and plane ticket?"

"In here." Dylan pointed to his computer bag.

"Get them out and keep them on your person." The driver opened the glove box and pointed to a stack of Xeroxed papers. "Most policemen required a fiche, a form containing your information and travel itinerary. I've taken the liberty of making some copies. At checkpoints, if you can hand them a copy, it saves time. Otherwise, they take you into an office and write down your information. Usually at a pretty leisurely pace."

Once the man locked Dylan's phone and laptop in back, they got underway. Military or police were reassuringly present almost everywhere. But after dealing with them at the first half-dozen checkpoints, he began to wonder if being detained by them wouldn't be as bad as by kidnappers. Sometimes Uthman had to pay a small bribe. Dylan never figured out how the man knew whether it was expected, but he was grateful to have an escort who clearly understood the ins and outs.

The farther they got from the capital, the fewer roads were paved. Finally, they were following dirt tracks into and out of small villages consisting of a couple dozen stone and brick buildings the same color as the road. The nicest building in a settlement was usually the mosque, and often that was simply a drab box with some tile work around the doorway and a minaret tower for the call to prayer. The temperature hovered at a brutal forty-four degrees centigrade— north of a hundred and twenty Fahrenheit—and shocked his system every time he stepped out of the air-conditioned vehicle.

It took them the rest of the day to reach the regional capital, Atar. Uthman pulled up to an ancient stone fort with a tall tower. "It's at least another three hours to the Richat. We'll spend the night here and go there first thing in the morning."

The fort, now named Hotel Lemina Mint Maata, was completely enclosed by a thick wall. It featured air-conditioned rooms and secure, private parking. Uthman said it was the safest place for hundreds of kilometers. Dylan had no doubt. The fifty-foot-tall tower had small square openings that he assumed had once served as gun ports. He could almost imagine French Legionnaires pointing their bolt-action carbines through them. A satellite dish atop the tower gave him hope the place would have Internet.

They bought rooms for two nights, so he could spend as long as he wanted at the Richat tomorrow and be assured of a place to sleep before the long drive back the following day.

Chapter 22
Eye of the Sahara, at Last

In the morning, they ate a hurried breakfast of fried flatbread and strong coffee, and then got underway. Dylan was antsy. Their route through the Amoijar Pass felt like he was being pinched between steep canyon walls. Beyond the pass, the rest of the way to Chinguetti and then Ouadane wasn't any easier.

Ouadane was a small modern settlement adjacent to the intact ruins of an ancient walled city of stone buildings. They stopped and bought enough food and water to last the day. By a well at the edge of the market, a herdsman watered a dozen camels from a trough. He proudly told them the well was thirty meters deep and maintained by the entire community—very similar to the wells he had been installing throughout Algeria. The man offered them fresh camel milk, which they politely declined, saying they'd just finished breakfast.

Long ago, Ouadane had been the staging post of the Trans-Saharan trade and for camels transporting slabs of salt. Caravans declined in the thirteenth century. Now it was a UNESCO World Heritage Site. If he had time, Dylan might explore it later. What was important now was that Ouadane sat on the edge of the Richat.

At last, he'd reached the Eye of the Sahara.

As soon as the Land Rover stopped moving, Dylan threw open his door, grabbed his hat, water bottle, and camera, and set off on foot. The view was truly astonishing. He saw the concentric rings, exactly as Plato had described them. From the satellite photos, he'd estimated them to be twenty-five miles in diameter. Obviously, he wasn't going to walk that far. Frankly, it was easier to see the rings from space than on the ground.

He made his way down into the nearest ravine. Early geologists theorized the Richart might be an impact crater, but a skilled geophysicist like Dylan could tell from the extrusive igneous rocks that it hadn't been formed by a meteor strike—no shatter pattern. He returned to the car to inform his driver that he was going farther into the Richat. He opened the sack of food they'd bought and put half in his backpack. He took extra water, too. He had the feeling the place was deserted enough that he didn't have to worry about being kidnapped.

He hiked toward the center, trying to find the right balance between hurrying to see as much as possible and going slow enough to not miss details. Some of the rocks were clearly hydrothermally altered, and the eroded remains of two shallow lakes known as maars were clear. If he had to guess, he'd estimate that about a hundred million years ago, the two concentric rings had formed by erosion. Acting like dikes, they'd trapped water as the level of the lakes dropped, creating natural canals.

The perfect place for an ancient civilization.

According to field maps, which he'd studied prior to coming, the inner ring, which lay three kilometers from an island in the center of the Richat, was twenty meters wide. The outer ring, in which he now stood, looked to be fifty meters wide. That'd make a generous natural canal, easy for Atlantis's founders to develop.

If the Atlanteans repurposed a geologic formation to suit their needs, he should be able to find evidence. They would have had to smooth the channels. There would have been bridges. Even wooden bridges might leave traces in the edge of the rock. Michael Hübner claimed to have found ancient stone houses made from the red, black, and white colored stones Plato mentioned. Where were they?

It was eight kilometers to the edge of what once would have been the center island. The walk there, over rugged terrain, took him almost two hours. Throughout the afternoon, he scoured the area, taking pictures of the edges of the canals, examining the rocks for any sign of being worked by tools. He found no trace of any building blocks. Of course, Hübner had warned that the colored stones were being carted off and sold to make paint pigment, and called for the area to be named a World Heritage site to protect it. If all the building materials had disappeared this quickly, UNESCO should have heeded his warning.

Dylan found plenty of stone tool artifacts—the place would be an archeologist's wet dream. But the Atlantis he was looking for would have evolved beyond primitive hand axes. Hübner had posited that these were buried artifacts from prehistoric times that were pushed to the surface in later upheavals or earthquakes.

After another hour of searching, the reality began to set in. He found no evidence of anything post-Neolithic.

To say he was disappointed that the site had been scavenged would be an understatement. He wished Hübner were here, walking him through what he'd found. The sunlight was waning and so was he. Making his way back to the Land Rover, he saw signs of torrential water flows. Among fine-grained deposits in their wake, he found a plethora of well-preserved freshwater fossils. He bagged some, intending to have them radiocarbon dated when he got home—at least he could establish that the canals had once held water. Legally, he couldn't remove artifacts. Then again, it wasn't legal for officers at checkpoints to collect bribes.

Dylan approached where he had entered the Richat, when he heard pop, pop, pop in rapid sequence. Gunfire? He ducked behind a stone ridgeline, at a loss for what to do. Call for help? How? His phone was in the

Land Rover. Besides, there likely wasn't a cell tower within miles of this place.

His mind leaped to the worse case—bandits had kidnapped his driver and stolen the vehicle. Could he make it back to Ouadane on foot? In the dark? With little water?

The sun dropped further behind the horizon. Its rays cast a long-fingered shadow of the Land Rover on the Richat's entrance. Dylan listened hard and was relieved when the faint purr of the engine met his ears. He slowly peeked over the crest of rock and saw Uthman standing outside the car, looking west.

"Uh, hello," Dylan said.

Uthman turned and waved. "Did you find what you came for, or do you want to come back here tomorrow?"

"Was there a problem? I thought I heard—"

"Gunfire? No, just a poorly maintained motor scooter ridden by a couple of local ruffians who came to see if we'd left anything valuable unlocked. Once I showed them I was armed, they rode away."

Thank God Asenath had hired him a bodyguard. Dylan climbed into the air-conditioned vehicle and slid low in his seat. "Let's go to the fort . . . er . . . hotel."

Uthman shifted into reverse, swung the Rover in a half circle, and headed in that direction. "So, are we coming back in the morning?"

"Can't. I'm on the red-eye tomorrow night. We should leave for the airport as soon as we get up, in case we get held up at as many checkpoints as we did on the way here."

"Wise man."

But was he? He'd dedicated too much of the last year to the Atlantis project, and what had he expected to find? The capstone of a pyramid, a palace decorated with red and black stones? He was one man wandering at random around a site that was thirty square miles in size.

He turned on his camera and scrolled through the photos he'd snapped. Nothing startling, nothing definitive. It wasn't a volcanic caldera, or a meteor crater. The Richat Structure was definitely unique and had once held water. But was it Atlantis? He had no more proof than he'd had before he came here. His next step should be to contact Michael Hübner. He might have photos from before the red and black stones were carried away. Or at least the location where they might have been taken.

He pulled out the plastic bag of fossils he'd collected and examined them. That wasn't really his field. He'd hand them off to a colleague when he returned to the University of Florida.

Did that mean he was going back to finish his doctorate? He guessed so. What else was there for him to do?

Uthman glanced at the bag. "Those sea shells?"

"Freshwater creatures, actually."

"Well, if you're interested, the desert in the Nouadhibou Region of Mauretania is covered with ancient whale bones. No one knows how they wound up so many miles inland. We could stop there on our way back."

Dylan smiled. "Thanks, but no. I saw a whole national park of whale fossils in Egypt." And if he'd never read about the Eye of the Sahara, he might not have chased Holly there. Another way the last six months had been wasted.

An hour later, the driver pulled through the gates of the old fort that served as their hotel and parked.

Fatigued and disappointed, Dylan ate a hurried supper and went to bed early.

Chapter 23
Change in Plans

Dylan rolled over and looked at the clock. His alarm wouldn't go off for another hour. He realized the morning call to prayer had woken him. He'd grown accustomed to it and most days could sleep through it. Not today. Maybe it was this cold stone fort, or maybe the frustration of not finding . . .

Unable to fall back asleep, he lay in his bed, thinking. Wasn't the Richat still the most likely site of Atlantis? Yes. He just didn't have any evidence. Why was he surprised? Atlantis existed 5,500 years ago, and a powerful tsunami would have washed it into the sea. That's what Plato said happened. Finally, he decided the thing to do was visit Michael Hübner on his way back to the States. Hübner might have photos or rock samples, something to build a dissertation on.

Asenath had bought him a refundable ticket. It wouldn't be that difficult to change it to include a stopover in Germany. He got out his laptop and logged onto the hotel's internet.

First, he had to find out what city Hübner lived in. He hoped it was near Frankfort. That would have the best connections. He googled "Michael Hübner."

Seven million links came up. At the top of the page was a Wikipedia entry—always a reliable source. He clicked it.

Michael Hübner, a German bicyclist. Wrong guy.

He clicked the back arrow and scrolled further down the search results. There were a lot of Germans named Michael Hübner.

He found a link to a page for Michael Hübner on Atlantipedia. It might not have his address, but at least it'd be the right Hübner. He clicked the link, and the page displayed, but Hübner wasn't at the top. Dylan scrolled down until he found him.

What? No!

The subhead read: "Hübner, Michael (1966-2013)."

"It can't be true." He scanned the subsequent paragraphs.

Shit. There it was. *"Tragically, Michael Hübner died in December 2013 as a result of a cycling accident."* Well, forget changing his ticket.

He disconnected his phone from the charger and brought up his contact list. He scrolled until he came to Holly Johnson's name. They hadn't spoken since the symposium and had exchanged just the one brief flurry of text messages six months ago. He had no idea what he'd say to her if he made the call. Besides, he'd just heard the call to prayer. It must be 4:30 in the morning. What time was it, wherever she was? He'd lost track of the time zones in northwestern Africa as surely as he'd lost track of her whereabouts.

Waking her in the wee hours wouldn't be a good start. A text would be better. If she were asleep, she'd see it when she woke. His thumbs flew over the keyboard, tapping out a long missive. He hit send, then reread what he'd written. Too much information. He regretted it immediately.

The phone vibrated in his hand. He looked at the screen. She'd sent a smiley face. What the hell did that mean?

He typed: "Did I wake you?"

"No, grading papers."

"What time is it where U R?"

"Midnight. Gainesville."

Gainesville! Had she been there this whole time? He texted back: "Can you talk now, or is it too late?"

"Call me."

He did.

During the two hours they talked, he logged onto the UF website and re-enrolled for the next semester. Then he sent an email to his advisor asking if he could find him a position as a teaching assistant. By the time the conversation got around to him, he could honestly say he was a UF doctoral student who had completed his course work and only needed to finish his dissertation. But this time he'd get it written.

Proof of Atlantis may be lost to him, but Holly wasn't. When he told her what he'd been doing with the NGO, she didn't scold him. She praised him for giving back. As he described his work, it dawned on him that a new dissertation topic could evolve from the work he'd done in Algeria. Holly had mentioned it in her presentation. She could point him toward academic research his committee would approve.

Dylan and Holly continued talking until she said, "Oh my God, look at the time. I've got to get to bed. I teach an eight o'clock class."

"I'll be home Friday. Can I see you that night?"

"If you're not too jet lagged."

"It won't matter if I am—Holly?"

"Yes, Dylan?"

"I really love you."

"I love you, too. I can't wait to see you. Bye."

Too excited to sleep, Dylan continued to troll the internet. He stumbled across a YouTube video, "Why is the CIA Hiding Something about an Advanced Civilization in the Sahara?" Well, he'd just come from there and hadn't seen anything for the CIA to hide. But he watched it anyway. When it finished, YouTube automatically played another video, and then another after that. Before the fourth one started, he stopped and switched to Amazon, looking for something to read on the long flight home.

While browsing, Amazon suggested a title, *Atlantis Dying* by Richard Gartee. He clicked on the cover image and scanned the book's summary. Next, he clicked the "Look Inside" feature and started reading. The book was fiction, but in the preface, the author cited the same scientists Dr. Porter and Professor Gujarat had in their symposium lectures so very long ago.

Michael Hübner showed up on the fourth page. Was this coincidence or a gift from the gods? How could he resist?

Luckily, there were both paperback and electronic versions. He clicked "Buy" and downloaded it to his Kindle.

There was a sharp rap on his door. Uthman said, "Time to go, Mr. Clarke."

He closed his laptop, unplugged it, and stuffed everything in his computer bag. "I'm ready."

And he was.

Chapter 24
Homecoming Confessions

The American Airlines commuter jet from Miami touched down and taxied to one of Gainesville Airport's three jetways. Dylan unbuckled his seatbelt, snatched his backpack from beneath the seat in front of him, and stood in the aisle. After he'd cleared customs in Miami, he'd texted Holly the arrival time of his flight to Gainesville and asked if she would pick him up. She'd replied with a thumbs-up and three heart emojis.

He was finally going to see her in the flesh.

He shifted his weight from foot to foot as his fellow passengers retrieved their belongings from the overhead compartments and chattered on their cell phones. And didn't move. His own phone battery was dead. He bent down and peered out the plane window, knowing it was impossible to see the opposite side of the lobby.

Tucked safely between two tee shirts in his backpack was a small box containing the expensive perfume he'd bought at the duty-free store during his layover at Lisbon airport.. The shop had racks of wine and liquor, display cases crammed with watches, and electronics. But he wanted a more romantic gift for Holly.

One counter sold high-end fragrances. A willowy Portuguese woman in her early twenties spritzed samples on strips of blotter paper, then waved them under Dylan's nose until he felt he couldn't tell the difference. He stepped away and analyzed the problem. Basically, there were classics —flowery, French, seductive, versus contemporary concoctions—sharp, lusty, with slightly chemical undertones.

Who was he kidding? Holly rarely wore perfume. The bottle would probably just gather dust. Still, between flowers, chocolate, or perfume, the latter conveyed intimacy. Even if she scarcely used it, a pretty crystal bottle on her dresser would remind her of him. He'd returned to the salesperson and told her to limit his choices to French classics.

The passengers in front of him finally began to move at a snail's pace. Once they exited the plane door, the throng spread out, and Dylan wove his way among them to the end of the jetway. He hurried across the open expanse of the airport waiting room, scanning the crowd on the other side of the glass wall. No Holly. He pushed through the revolving door, eager to open his arms and enfold her.

Where was she? The arriving passenger area wasn't large enough to hide her. He circled it twice, threading his way amidst hugging, smiling families and lovers. No sign of her. Had she had second thoughts?

An announcement on the PA said passengers arriving from Miami could now claim their luggage in the baggage area.

Gainesville's baggage claim consisted of a single conveyor belt. Dylan's fellow passengers crowded around it, watching a square opening in the wall at the far end, waiting for suitcases to appear. Finally, bags of various sizes and color began to stream out the opening. People jostled one another, trying to yank their suitcase off the belt before it passed them. Dylan waited at the back of the crowd, looking over their heads for his dusty brown rollaboard.

"Hey, stranger."

Dylan spun around, his backpack jostling the man next to him. "Sorry."

There she was.

He wrapped his arms around her, lifted her off her feet, and kissed her.

"Sorry I wasn't here when you landed," she said when he let her breathe again. "It took forever to find a spot in short-term parking."

Dylan felt like his face could break from smiling. "You are a sight for sore eyes."

"Is that your only bag?"

"No. I'm waiting for mine to come out." He checked the conveyor just as his suitcase disappeared back into the wall. "Well, it'll come around again."

They held hands until it reappeared. Then he grabbed it and they walked to the parking lot, hand in hand.

"Are you jetlagged?" she said.

"Just the opposite. I'm so stoked at seeing you, I couldn't sleep if I tried."

She squeezed his hand. "That's sweet. Well then, how about a home cooked meal?"

"Sounds perfect."

Leaving the airport, Holly cruised along, managing to catch green lights all the way across town. "You haven't seen my new apartment," she said. "It's nice. Away from the student complexes. More adults—instructors, single professionals. I felt once a person has her doctorate and a teaching position, she doesn't exactly belong in the undergrad scene."

Dylan glanced her way and squirmed in his seat.

"Oh, I didn't mean . . . You'll definitely finish your PhD. Understand, I was just talking about me. You can live wherever.

"No, what you say makes sense." Dylan squirmed some more. "I . . . uh . . . er . . . Actually, I was hoping I could crash with you for a few days. You see, I sublet my apartment when I left for Africa, and the tenants are still in it."

She smiled. "Of course you can. As a matter of fact, I intended to invite you to sleep over after we ate supper."

Well. Could this day get any better?

Holly's new place was in a cluster of four new duplexes surrounded by stands of tall pine with the obligatory palm tree at the entrance.

Dylan carried his luggage in from the car while she unlocked the door. "Do you mind if I take a shower?"

"Not at all. The bathroom is through the bedroom."

He dropped his bags inside the door, took her in his arms, and gave her a long kiss. "You have no idea how much I've missed you. Let's eat later. Why don't you show me that shower?"

Holly pulled off her tee shirt. "Right this way."

They hooked up first, then took a shower, then made love again. It was both fresh and new, and old and familiar. Sex was never better than between people who knew each other well.

After the second go round, Holly rolled off of him and lay on her side of the bed panting. "Whew! I thought after flying night and day, you'd be exhausted."

"Well, I've been saving myself for you."

She turned and looked into his eyes. "Me, too. I haven't been with anybody since we hooked up at the symposium." Holly swung her feet off the bed and stood up. "I'll be right back." She slipped into the bathroom and closed the door.

While she was gone, Dylan got his backpack, retrieved her gift, set it on her pillow, lay back down, and waited.

Holly came out of the bath smiling. "It might be too late to start the elaborate meal I had planned, but if you're starved, I can whip up something simpler in a heartbeat."

Dylan reached for her. "Come back to bed."

"Much as I'd like that—" Her eyes fell on the box. "Chanel No. 5! Dylan, you shouldn't have!" She jumped on the bed and opened the package. Inside was a small bottle with a crystal cap.

"I know you seldom wear cologne," Dylan said, "but I wanted to bring you something, and the bottle is pretty."

"Dylan, this isn't cologne. This is eau de parfum! It's a lovely gift. Thank you." She kissed him, sat up, removed the top, and sprayed just a little on her throat and between her breasts.

A floral aroma with an aphrodisiac undertone surrounded them. Holly nuzzled his neck. "What do you think?"

"It smells completely different on you than it did in the store."

"Good or bad."

"Fantastically good. Sensual. Seductive."

Holly smiled and cuddled next to him. And that's how they both drifted off to sleep.

* * *

Dylan opened his eyes to find Holly watching him. Sunlight streamed through the window from a high angle. "Don't you teach mornings?"

"It's Saturday."

"It is? I guess I really lost track of my days." He kissed her. "Good morning." The Chanel fragrance still lingered. "You smell really nice."

"Thanks to you." She kissed him again. "I'm famished. Let's shower and then make breakfast."

"Sounds like a plan." It had been less than one day, and already being with Holly felt easy and natural.

After they'd showered, she scrambled eggs with cream cheese and chives. Dylan toasted English muffins and set the table.

"There's apple butter in the refrigerator," she said.

He put the jar on the table and buttered the muffins. She spooned equal portions of eggs on their plates and joined him at the table.

"This feels incredibly familiar," he said. "In all the best ways."

She looked away and busied herself spreading apple butter on her muffin until she'd evenly coated every cranny. He'd seen it before. Her avoidance behavior.

"Holly? What's wrong?"

She met his eyes. "I have a confession. After we reconnected at the symposium, I started thinking that when I returned to Gainesville, we might live together in our old apartment. When I got here and learned you'd left . . . I didn't know where we stood."

"I can sympathize. I remember arriving in Egypt and discovering that your contract was up. But why didn't you call or email? You answered a couple of texts, then nothing for months."

Holly blushed. "Well, I kind of felt foolish, thinking that we could just pick up again where we left off. And it isn't like I heard from you either . . ."

"Well, you know what it's like trying to get a signal out in the desert." Dylan stopped talking. This was the wrong way to make a fresh start. "No, you're right. Truth is, I was embarrassed at how impulsively I'd acted, and a little afraid you'd be pissed at me for running off to Africa."

He stroked Holly's hand. "Your idea of picking up where we left off isn't foolish. We didn't break up because we had problems. We were just living on different continents. Now that you're back and I'm back—"

"And you are finally going to finish your PhD."

"I am. I've already contacted Dr. Gujarat about a TA position."

Holly smiled. "A man with a degree and a job—now that's boyfriend material."

"Seriously," Dylan said, "my experience in North Africa gave me an idea I think my department will accept with no problem. Actually, the idea sprung from something in your presentation at the symposium."

"Don't keep me in suspense."

"My dissertation is going to contrast the benefits of community wells and small gardens in desert regions versus the detrimental impact of large-scale commercial agriculture operations that pump water from ten-thousand-year-old underground lakes. . . You know Asenath Kamel?"

"Of course."

"She has a ton of supporting research I can use."

"So do I. And I'll help you with the data analysis."

"That would be wonderful." Her statistics were always stronger than his. "Anyhow, I won't limit it just to the water issue. I'm expanding my dissertation to include the environmental consequences of massive fields of irrigated crops on the climate of the surrounding desert."

Holly picked up their plates and refilled their coffee. "So . . did you find Atlantis?"

Dylan had vowed not to mention Atlantis. But since she'd brought it up, he couldn't be blamed. "I did get to explore the Eye of the Sahara before I left Africa. I have photos if you'd like to see them. I admit I didn't find proof that it was the place. But the topography of the Richat structure certainly fits Plato's description. Unfortunately, the researcher who wrote the original paper on it has died, and blocks of colored stone he cited as evidence have since been scavenged and ground into pigment."

"Is that enough for you?"

Dylan shrugged. "It has to be. I went. I saw. I didn't conquer. I don't know there is anything more for me to do."

"If you're satisfied, that's good."

"I did read an interesting novel set in Atlantis on the flight home that made me think about the Egyptian pyramids."

Holly rolled her eyes.

"No, listen. I'm sure you visited the pyramids while you were in Cairo. Asenath said she takes everyone."

Holly nodded. "We even went inside, up to the King's Chamber."

Dylan shivered. "Oh, wasn't that an experience?"

She paused for a long time. "Uh . . . did you touch the sarcophagus?"

"You mean it happened to you, too?"

She nodded.

"Asenath thinks it's the focal point of some sort of subtle energy field."

"Well, I definitely felt something," she said. "It was pretty amazing,"

"Anyway, this novel, *Atlantis Dying*, made me question where the Egyptians got the math and geometry required to build such precise pyramids. What if Atlantis *was* the Eye of the Sahara, and when it fell, some of the Atlantean refugees made their way east to the Nile?"

"Oh, Dylan, you just said you were done obsessing about Atlantis."

"I am, I am. Starting Monday, I'm going to find a place to live until my tenants' sublet ends, and write, write, write on my dissertation."

Holly came over and hugged him. "You have a place here. Forget our old apartment. Let's live together again."

"You mean it?"

She sat on his lap and kissed him. "I do. This afternoon, let's get your things out of storage and bring them here."

He hadn't found Atlantis, but he had a fresh start with Holly. It couldn't get any better than that.

The End

Author's Note

Since the days of Plato, people have searched for and argued over possible locations for Atlantis. What little we know of Atlantis comes to us through Plato, who claimed the source of his information was the great Greek statesman, Solon, who first learned of Atlantis while visiting a temple in ancient Egypt.

Plato passed on many exacting details about the size of Atlantis and its whereabouts. One clue searchers ignored was his statement that Atlantis was larger than Libya. In the same passage, he also said that Atlantis ruled over several other islands, over parts of the continent, and had subjected parts of Libya.

An even earlier Greek reference to Atlantis is found on a map created by the first historian and geographer, Herodotus, who lived about sixty years before Plato. His map, showing the known world of his time, accurately positioned the Atlas Mountains in northwest Africa. Adjacent lands south and east of them, he labeled "Atlantis."

Until the late twentieth century, the Sahara was thought to have been the way it is now for at least three million years. Then, in 1956, French oil exploration discovered vast quantities of fresh water two hundred feet below.

Twenty-five years later, NASA used a new type of ground-penetrating radar to scan a forty-eight-kilometer-wide swath of the Sahara from outer space. The scan revealed a buried network of ancient waterways crisscrossing the desert.

In 1995, oceanographer and paleoclimatologist, Peter deMenocal, published a scientific analysis of core samples extracted from the ocean floor off the coast of North Africa. The core samples showed that the Sahara had switched from wet to dry regularly every 20,000 years.

Satellites and NASA technology provide new tools for discovering previously unknown geological and archeological sites. Yet with billions of satellite images to sort through, it helps if you know where to look. That's where German researcher, Michael Hübner's algorithms came into play.

Michael Hübner created computer algorithms to refine a range of geographical details and other data. His result identified a site in the Republic of Mauritania, a country in northwest Africa near the Atlas Mountains and in the area Herodotus had labeled Atlantis. When Hübner checked photos on Google Earth, he spotted the Richat, or Eye of the Sahara, exactly where his calculations pointed. It was a caldera-like structure with unique characteristics: a central hill, surrounded by concentric rings that appeared to be dry riverbeds, and a deep crevice that extended out to the Atlantic Ocean, terminating in the possible remains of a harbor. Hübner traveled there and found the specific geomorphological formations and ruins of ancient buildings built from white, red, and black stones that matched Plato's details.

This book is a work of fiction. However, these and other scientific studies mentioned in the fictional symposium and elsewhere in the story are actual findings reported in reputable journals by the scientists named. They are listed in the bibliography below. Also several resources about Atlantis are included in the bibliography for interested readers.

Bibliography

Adams, Mark, *Meet Me in Atlantis: Across Three Continents in Search of the Legendary Sunken City*, New York: Dutton, 2015

Bonsor, Helen, et al, "Potential Impact of Climate Change on Improved and Unimproved Water Supplies in Africa," *Issues in Environmental Science and Technology*, Royal Society of Chemistry, London, August 2010.

Davidovits, Joseph, *The Pyramids: An Enigma Solved*, New York: Hippocrene Books, 1988

deMenocal, Peter B., "Pilo-Pleistocene African Climate," *Science*, New Series, Volume 270, Issue 5233, pp. 53-59, Oct. 6. 1995

Drake, Nick, et al, "Three North African dust source areas and their geochemical fingerprint," *Earth and Planetary Science Letters,* Volume 554, London: King's College, Jan. 15, 2021.

Hassan, Fekri, *Droughts, Food and Culture: Ecological Change and Food Security in Africa's Later Prehistory,* New York: Springer, 2007 updated 2002

Hübner, Michael, *Circumstantial Evidence for Plato's Island Atlantis in the Souss-Massa plain in today's South-Morocco,* Germany: asalas.org, 2008 updated 2012 https://web.archive.org/web/20190325094903/http://asalas .com/doku.php

Hübner, Michael, and Hübner, Sebastian, *New Evidence for a Large Prehistoric Settlement in a Caldera-Like Geomorphological Structure in Southwest Morocco*, Germany: asalas.org, 2012 https://web.archive.org /web/20190325094903/http://asalas.com/doku.php

O'Connell, Tony, *Atlantipedia: An A–Z Guide to the Search for Plato's Atlantis,* (a well-organized website for researching all things Atlantis) https://atlantipedia.ie

Plato, *Critias*, translated by Benjamin Jowett, New York: Scribner's Sons, 1871

Plato, *Timaeus*, translated by Benjamin Jowett, New York: Scribner's Sons, 1871

You may also enjoy . . .
Atlantis Dying

Ours isn't the first time politicians disregarded a climate crisis.

Despite the similarity of titles, *Atlantis Obsession* is not a sequel to *Atlantis Dying*. Although both stories make points about climate change, *Atlantis Obsession* takes place in present day, while *Atlantis Dying* is set 5,500 years ago.

When a change in the tilt of Earth's axis causes climate patterns to shift, Atlantis's experts warn that in a hundred years, their lush land will become a desert. To save their civilization, the king must relocate a million people to the Atlantean colonies. But greedy barons who control the corrupt Legislative Plenum want a wall to prevent migrating workers from reaching the ships.

Darmon, First Consul to the King, knows the entire population won't fit in the current colonies, and Atlanteans, accustomed to the free energy supplied by Tuaoi crystals, won't live anywhere that doesn't have one.

Then a techgnosic breakthrough creates the first new Tuaoi in millenniums. With it, Atlantis can establish another colony. Darmon sets sail to find a site. While he's away, things go from bad to worse. The barons get their wall. Next, they construct aqueducts to drain vast lakes, despite being warned that it will hasten desertification.

The drought worsens, yet powerful factions continue to disregard the undeniable evidence, even as the desert envelops the capital. The wall forces the poor to flee the encroaching desert on foot.

Darmon's wife, Hathorah, a teacher at the Mystery School, is tasked with choosing a colony for the school. She and Darmon put to sea with a team of techgnosists to deliver the new Tuaoi.

A fierce storm forces their ship to take refuge in a river delta where they discover Atlantean farmers who'd fled overland. But it was far more than a storm, as they discover when they return to Atlantis.

Or what's left of it.

A complete list of his available titles, upcoming events, and forthcoming books is available at www.gartee.com where you can also sign up to receive updates on his newest publications as they become available.

Also, please take a moment to leave a short review on Amazon and/or other booksellers' websites. Reviews help to sell books, and sales help an author to keep writing. You can readily find links to online booksellers' websites by visiting www.gartee.com and clicking on the book cover image.